GIFTED

Out of Sight
Out of Mind

Coming soon:
Gifted: Better Late Than Never

Look out for:
Gifted: Here Today, Gone Tomorrow
and more books in the GIFTED *series*

GIFTED

Out of Sight
Out of Mind

MARILYN KAYE

MACMILLAN CHILDREN'S BOOKS

First published 2009 by Kingfisher

This edition published 2009 by Macmillan Children's Books
a division of Macmillan Publishers Limited
20 New Wharf Road, London N1 9RR
Basingstoke and Oxford
Associated companies throughout the world
www.panmacmillan.com

ISBN 978-0-330-51036-3

3 5 7 9 8 6 4

A CIP catalogue record for this book is available from the British Library.

Printed and bound in the UK by CPI Mackays, Chatham, ME5 8TD

For my friends who first heard this story on the beach at Bandol: Thomas and Augustin Clerc, Emilie and Marion Grimaud, Jeanne, Angèle and Baptiste Latil, Liona, Fanny and Alice Lutz, je vous embrasse!

PROLOGUE

SOMETIMES I LOOK IN *a mirror and there's nobody looking back. I know I have a reflection. I just don't see it.*

Maybe it's all in my mind.

Maybe I've got bad eyesight.

Or maybe it's something else.

My name is Tracey. Tracey Devon. Did you get that? TRACEY DEVON. I'm writing this all in capital letters because it's like talking really loud. People might pay more attention.

I never speak loudly. In fact, I make very little noise at all. I'm a quiet person. When I talk, I whisper. When I laugh — which isn't very often — it's a silent laugh. When I cry, I can feel the tears on my face, but there's no sound.

I'm not a ghost. I'm a living, breathing, flesh-and-blood thirteen-year-old girl. All my senses are intact. I have two arms, two legs, a heart, a brain — all the usual stuff. I've got two eyes, two ears, one nose, one mouth — and they're all in the right places. I eat, drink, sleep, and use the toilet, just like everyone else.

But sometimes I look in a mirror and I don't see anyone looking back.

Maybe it's my imagination.

Maybe I'm going blind.

Or maybe I'm not really here at all.

CHAPTER ONE

THERE WERE 342 STUDENTS at Meadowbrook Middle School, and three lunch breaks each day. This meant that during any one lunch break, there could be no more than 114 students in the canteen. The noise and commotion, however, suggested that half the population of mainland China was eating lunch together.

Students roamed the cavernous space, shouting, racing from one end to the other, knocking over chairs, banging trays down on tables. There were a couple of teachers who were supposed to be supervising the scene and maintaining order, but they couldn't stop the occasional flying meatball from that day's Spaghetti Special or the far-reaching spray from a fizzy drink bottle that had been intentionally shaken before being opened.

From her prime seat at the best table, Amanda Beeson surveyed the chaotic scene with a sense of well-being. The canteen was noisy and messy and not very attractive, but it was part of her little kingdom – or queendom, if such a word existed. She wasn't wearing any kind of crown, of course, but she felt secure in the knowledge that in this particular hive, she was generally acknowledged as the queen bee.

On either side of her sat two princesses – Sophie Greene and Britney Teller. The three of them were about to begin their daily assessment of classmates. As always, Amanda kicked off the conversation. 'Ohmigod, check out Caroline's sweater! It's way too tight.'

'No kidding,' Sophie said. 'It's like she's begging for the boys to look at her.'

'And it's not like she's got anything on top to look *at*,' Britney added.

Amanda looked around for more victims. 'Someone should tell Shannon Fields that girls with fat knees shouldn't wear short skirts.'

'Terri Boyd has a new bag,' Britney pointed

out. 'Is it a Coach?'

Amanda shook her head. 'No way. It's a fake.'

'How can you tell from this far away?' Sophie wanted to know.

Amanda gave her a withering look. 'Oh, puh-leeze! Coach doesn't make hobo bags in lime green.' Spotting imitation designer goods was a favourite game, and Amanda surveyed the crowd for another example. 'Look at Cara Winters' sweater.'

'Juicy Couture?' Sophie wondered.

'*Not.* You can tell by the buttons.'

Sophie gazed at her with admiration. Amanda responded by looking pointedly at the item in Sophie's hand. 'Sophie, are you actually going to eat that cupcake? I thought you were on a diet.'

Sophie sighed, and pushed the cupcake to the edge of her tray. Amanda turned to her other side.

'Why are you staring at me like that?' Britney asked.

'You've got a major zit coming out on your chin.'

Britney whipped a mirror out of her bag.

'It's not that big,' Sophie assured her. 'No one can see it.'

'*I* can,' Amanda declared.

'Really?' Britney stared harder into the mirror. Amanda thought she saw her lower lip tremble and for a moment she almost felt sorry for her. Everyone knew that Britney was obsessed with her complexion. She was constantly searching her reflection for any evidence of an imminent breakout, she spent half her allowance on face creams, and she even saw a skin doctor once a month. Not that she really needed to give her skin all that attention. If Britney's face had been half as bad as she thought it was, she wouldn't be sitting at Amanda's table. But she was still staring into her little mirror, and now Amanda could see her eyes getting watery.

Oh no, don't let her cry, she thought. Amanda didn't like public displays of emotion. She was always afraid she'd get caught up in them herself.

Three more of their friends – Emma, Katie and Nina – joined them at the table, and Britney got more reassurance on the state of her skin. Finally, Amanda gave in. 'You know, I think there's a smudge on one of my contact lenses. Everybody looks like they've got zits.'

Britney looked relieved, and Amanda made a mental note not to waste insults on friends. She didn't want to have to feel bad about anything she said. Feelings could be so dangerous.

Luckily, Emma brought up a new subject. 'Heather Todd got a haircut.'

'From Budget Scissors,' Amanda declared, referring to a chain of cheap hair whackers.

'Really?'

'That's what it looks like.'

Katie giggled. 'Amanda, you're terrible!'

Amanda knew this was intended as a compliment and she accepted it by smiling graciously. Katie beamed in the aura of the smile, and Amanda decided not to mention the fact that Katie's tinted lipgloss had smeared.

Besides, there were so many others more deserving of her critical attention. Like the girl who was walking towards their table right now: Tracey Devon, the dreariest girl in the eighth grade, the most pathetic creature in the entire class – maybe even in the whole school.

In Amanda's experience, in all honesty, she knew that even the most deeply flawed individuals had *something* of value about them. A complete social nerd might be a brain, an ugly guy could be a great athlete, an enormously fat girl might have a nice singing voice. But Tracey Devon had absolutely nothing going for her.

She was thin – not in a top-model way, but so scrawny and bony that her elbows and knees looked abnormally large. No hips and, worse, no boobs.

She didn't shave her legs. The fact that she was blonde and the hairs barely showed was beside the point. Every girl Amanda knew started shaving her legs at the age of 11. Then there was the hair on her head – flat, stringy and always looking in need of a wash. Her face was bland and colourless, she had no eyebrows to speak of, and her lips were so thin she looked like she didn't have a mouth either. The best anyone could say about her face was that she didn't have zits – but she had enough freckles to make up for that.

As for her clothes – forget designer stuff, Tracey's outfits went beyond terrible. Mismatched tops and bottoms, puffed-sleeve dresses that looked like they were made for five-year-olds, shoes with laces, and ankle socks. Socks!

And that wasn't all. Tracey's special and unique ickiness went way beyond the surface. She walked around with her shoulders hunched and her head bowed. She talked in whispers – people could barely hear her, and when they did, she never seemed to say anything worth hearing. It was like she wasn't even *there*, wherever she was.

But at that very moment she was definitely at their table, and Amanda stiffened. 'What do *you* want?' she demanded.

Tracey mumbled something, but the only word Amanda caught was 'Katie'. She called to the other end of the table. 'Katie, your new best friend, Tracey Devon, needs to talk to you.'

Katie's brow furrowed. 'Who?'

'Tracey Devon! Are you blind? She's standing right here.'

Katie glanced at the unwelcome visitor vaguely. 'Oh, right. What do you want?'

Somehow, Tracey managed to make her request

audible. 'Could I borrow your notes from yesterday?'

Katie still looked puzzled. 'Notes for what? Are you in one of my classes?'

'History,' Tracey said in a whisper.

'Oh yeah, right. Why do you need my notes?'

'I wasn't in class. I was sick.'

'Sick,' Amanda repeated. 'That's interesting. I didn't know ugliness was a disease.'

It wasn't one of her best wisecracks, but it got a response from Tracey. She raised her head just high enough for Amanda and the others to see the flush that crossed her face and the tears welling up in her eyes. Then she turned and scurried away.

'I just remembered – she's borrowed my notes before,' Katie remarked.

A flicker of concern crossed Britney's face. 'Is she sick a lot?'

Katie shrugged. 'Who knows? I never notice if she's there or not. It's like she's one of those people you don't see.' She took a bite of her sandwich, and the others followed.

But Amanda couldn't eat. She was too – too something. Angry? Maybe. Because it was so infuriating, the way Tracey was. It was her own fault that Amanda could mock her so easily. It was like she *wanted* to be picked on. She didn't make the slightest effort to improve herself, and she just took Amanda's insults without making any attempt at retaliation. There were plenty of other creepy types at Meadowbrook, but at least they stood up for themselves. Like Jenna Kelley, the girl who dressed in black and had a terrible reputation. If you accused her of being a vampire, she'd tell you where to go. Why didn't Tracey ever fight back?

Her friends had gone back to eating and chatting by now. Clearly they'd forgotten all about Tracey's interruption. They probably considered Tracey beneath their contempt, not even worth an insult. Only Amanda was still seething.

She clenched her fists. Uh-oh! This wasn't good. She could feel her face getting warm and her heartbeat quickening. *Too much feeling.*

'I've got to get something from my locker,' she muttered to the others. Before anyone could respond, she turned and hurried to the exit. She didn't have a hall pass, and if a monitor spotted her she could be hauled to the principal's office, but she had to risk it.

Luckily, she was able to make it to the end of the hall and down two flights of stairs to the school basement without being caught. There was a rarely used bathroom there, and she ducked into it. Splashing some water on her face, she gripped the sides of the sink, stared into the mirror, and concentrated on pushing any sympathy, any anger − any feelings at all for Tracey Devon − out of her head.

Do not feel sorry for her, she ordered herself. *She doesn't deserve any sympathy.*

Actually, Amanda knew that if someone *wanted* to take pity on Tracey Devon, she wouldn't care. But that someone could not be Amanda Beeson. She knew too well the terrible consequences of caring. And to make sure she remembered, she allowed the memories to play out in her head.

The very first time . . . she couldn't have been more than five. She saw herself on a cold winter afternoon, walking along a busy shopping street, clutching her mother's hand and looking at the people they passed. One in particular grabbed her attention.

She was huddled in the entrance of an old abandoned building, her back against the boarded door. A bowl with a few coins in it lay beside her, and there was a hand-scrawled sign propped against the wall. Wispy grey hair poked out of a dirty bandanna that was wrapped around her head. Her body was clothed in filthy rags, and even though Amanda wasn't close enough to smell her, she somehow knew that the woman exuded a nasty odour. And even though she couldn't read the sign, she knew the woman was hungry.

Amanda's mother hadn't noticed her, but she had paused in front of the shop window next to the building. Something in the display must have caught her eye, because she spent some time looking at it, which gave little Amanda more time to look at the poor woman.

Now, eight years later, she could still remember what she felt – sad, unbearably sad, sadder than she'd felt when her pet goldfish died. Why did this woman have to sit there in the cold, all alone? Didn't she have any family? Didn't anyone love her? That poor woman! What was she feeling?

Then, suddenly, she knew what the woman was feeling. Because she *was* the woman. Cold and hungry, and confused, too. And she was looking at a little girl – a pretty five-year-old, with long, glossy hair topped by a woolly hat. Sturdy, bright-eyed and wrapped in a puffy jacket. Holding the hand of a well-dressed, elegant woman in a fur coat.

And if Amanda had turned into the old lady, who was the little girl staring at her?

Her mother spoke. 'Amanda, where are your gloves?'

'They're in my pocket,' the little girl replied in Amanda's very own voice.

'Put them on. It's getting cold,' her mother said.

'OK.' She took her gloves out of her pocket and put them on, just as Amanda would do. Amanda-the-old-lady was bewildered. So, she was here – and she was there. How could that be?

In the turmoil of her confused mind, there were feelings that stood out – envy, longing, loneliness – oh, it was so awful being this woman,

Amanda couldn't bear it!

It only took a jerk of her mother's hand to pull her back into herself. In the next moment she was on a street corner at her mother's side, waiting for the light to change. She knew the sad woman was just behind her, but she didn't dare turn back to look.

The next time it happened she was older – eight or nine. It must have been summer, because she was in the back garden, wearing shorts and a vest top, having a picnic with a couple of friends. From the house next door came the sound of two people shouting at each other. Amanda recognized the voices even before the man and woman emerged – Mr Blakely first, followed by Mrs Blakely. Amanda liked Mrs Blakely – she had a little baby boy, and sometimes she let Amanda hold him. Mr Blakely wasn't as friendly. Just then, Mr Blakely looked very angry, and Mrs Blakely looked scared. Then, to Amanda's horror, Mr Blakely hit Mrs Blakely – he slapped her right across the face – and Mrs Blakely started to cry.

It was awful – Amanda had never seen an adult

cry like that before. How could that mean Mr Blakely do that? And why didn't Mrs Blakely hit him back? Nice Mrs Blakely, who baked chocolate-chip cookies and sang to her baby and promised Amanda she could babysit for him when she was old enough! Why was this happening? What could she do? What was Mrs Blakely going to do?

Nothing. Because her husband was stronger, and angry, and even though he hit her sometimes, she loved him so much and she was so afraid he'd leave her alone with the baby . . . Amanda knew all this because she had become Mrs Blakely, and when Mr Blakely hit her again, it was Amanda who felt the sting on her cheek. It was terrible; she was in pain, and just over the hedge she could see two little girls watching in horror along with Amanda, who didn't look upset in the least. It was like she didn't have any feelings at all. Which made a weird kind of sense, because the Amanda-with-feelings was in the body of Mrs Blakely.

The rest of the memory was a blur, but somehow Amanda got back into her own body. Soon after that, Mr and Mrs Blakely moved house.

There were other experiences. Two stood out – that time in the fifth grade when she saw a classmate get hit by a car in front of the school and then felt herself lying on the street, frightened and in pain and hearing the sound of the ambulance. And another time, just three years ago, when she became a *boy* – a skinny, nerdy, whiny boy named Martin, younger than her, who lived across the street. Nobody in the neighbourhood liked Martin, and his mother was always complaining to other mothers about the way their kids treated him. But then one day she saw him surrounded by bigger boys, who were pushing him back and forth and laughing at him, and she felt sorry for him . . .

That was the last one. Because by then, she'd worked it out. Feeling too much – that was the problem. When she felt bad for someone else, that was when it happened. Now, at the age of thirteen, she knew the words: sympathy, compassion, pity. Those were the emotions that triggered the bizarre bodysnatching, that transported her into other people and made her feel what they were feeling.

Once she'd understood, she knew what she had to do to prevent it from happening again. She had to stop feeling these emotions. If she didn't care about someone, she wouldn't become that person.

So she stopped caring. It wasn't easy, and often she had to struggle, but it was worth it so that she never had to suffer the experience again. At first she just tried to block the feelings of sympathy, but then she realized it would be useful to actually fight them. She focused on behaviour that would work contrary to compassion – mockery, ridicule, creative insults. And in the process she discovered a strange truth – people admired her meanness, or else they were just frightened of her. In any case, it worked to her advantage.

And now she had a fabulous life. She was the Queen of Mean and she ruled the school – or at least the eighth grade, though she felt pretty sure that her fame extended to the younger grades. She was never alone; classmates sought her approval and she was held in awe. She knew there were people who claimed to hate her, but she had no doubt that what they really wanted was to *be* her.

After a few deep breaths, another splash of water on the face and a quick make-up repair, she was ready to go back to the canteen and pick up where she'd left off. And she made it through the day without feeling sorry for anyone again.

But later that night, in her beautiful pink-and-white bedroom, lying in her four-poster bed under a lacy canopy, Amanda thought about the strange event of the day and wondered how it had come to pass. Why had she felt a glimmer of pity for Tracey Devon? True, Tracey was pathetic, but she wasn't a victim like Mrs Blakely or the girl who had been hit by the car.

What did she know about Tracey anyway? Not much. She knew that Tracey was one of those 'gifted' kids who attended a special class at Meadowbrook. Which was sort of hard to believe, because she didn't strike Amanda as being any kind of genius. They'd gone to the same primary school, and Tracey had been in Amanda's second-grade class. They weren't best friends – she was just another classmate – but there had been nothing especially awful about her. Tracey was OK back then.

In fact, she was almost famous. Everyone in town was talking about Tracey's family that year – her mother had just given birth to septuplets, seven identical baby girls. They were on TV, on the news. The 'Devon Seven' – that's what the reporters called them. The babies were in ads, and they posed for newspaper pictures, and every year after that the TV news included a special report showing them on their birthday. They were famous, the 'Devon Seven'.

But not Tracey Devon. She wasn't on those special TV shows. That wasn't surprising, in Amanda's opinion. Who would want to see a nerd like Tracey on TV?

Amanda realized then what really annoyed her – the fact that Tracey didn't *have* to be a nerd. She didn't have to dress so badly or act so nervous. Why didn't she stand up for herself? Why did she take all the abuse everyone heaped on her? She was more than a nerd – she was a wimp, never fighting back, not even *trying*. She was a total, complete, absolute *loser* . . .

Amanda was aware of beads of sweat forming on her forehead. She was getting all worked up again.

This wouldn't do at all. She couldn't let Tracey bother her. Everyone else just ignored her, so why couldn't she?

She had to calm down or she'd never get to sleep.

She did sleep finally. When she next opened her eyes, there was sunlight pouring in the window . . . which was odd, because her mother always woke her up when she came in to open the shutters on Amanda's windows. But there was no one else in the room . . .

She blinked. Where was her canopy? Why was she looking at a ceiling? Had she fallen off her bed? Because this didn't feel like her bed – it was harder. As her eyes began to focus, the first real stirrings of fear began. She noticed the chest of drawers in front of her. It was yellow, not pink. And what were those flowered curtains doing at the sides of her window? No . . . not *her* window. Not her room.

She sat up suddenly, and that was when she noticed her hands. What had happened to her manicure – the nice rosy polish? Whose stubby, bitten fingernails were these?

Her heart was pounding furiously, but her body

moved in slow motion. Lifting legs that weren't her legs. Putting feet on the floor, experiencing the new sensation of a carpet instead of a fluffy rug. Walking towards a mirror that hung above the unfamiliar chest of drawers. Looking in the mirror and seeing . . .

Tracey Devon.

CHAPTER TWO

THE REFLECTION STARED BACK at her, frozen and uncomprehending. The same pale freckled face, greasy hair and thin lips she'd scorned the day before in the canteen. The scrawny body, barely concealed by a thin, babyish nightgown covered in faded pink flowers. There was no question about it – Amanda Beeson *was* Tracey Devon.

Her body couldn't move, but her insides were shaking. Amanda closed her eyes. *Think of who you really are*, she commanded herself. Amanda Beeson, five foot two, 110 pounds, light brown hair, blue eyes, turned-up nose. Amanda Beeson, the coolest girl at Meadowbrook Middle School, the Queen of Mean. Frantically, she tried to remember what she'd worn to bed the previous night: an extra-large T-shirt with 'I heart New York' written on it that her father had brought back for her from his last business trip. When she had the image firmly imprinted in her mind, she opened her eyes again. The shock she was feeling was still visible on the face of Tracey Devon.

The silence of the room was broken by a series of harsh beeps. It took Amanda a moment to realize that the noises were coming from an alarm clock on the beside table. She turned it off and sat down on the bed.

Stay calm, she told herself. *You know what's happening. It's happened before and it will pass.* She was actually more angry than frightened. Damn that Tracey Devon for demanding pity! If Amanda had disliked the girl before, she positively hated her now. *Hate, hate, hate*, she repeated silently.

Surely you couldn't feel sympathy for someone you hated. If she concentrated on her real feelings for Tracey, she'd get out of Tracey's body and back into her own.

But it was hard to focus on hate when what she was really feeling at the moment was hunger. It occurred to her that maybe her hunger was making her too weak to get back into herself.

She could do something about that.

Moving awkwardly on unfamiliar feet, she went to the door and out into the hallway. So this was Tracey's house – or at least, the upstairs part of it. She heard voices coming from another room and edged along the wall to peek in and see what was going on inside.

She recognized the seven little girls immediately from pictures in magazines. The Devon Seven were getting dressed, assisted by a weary-looking woman – Tracey's mother? – and a teenage girl. Did Tracey have an older sister?

'Lizzie, help Sandie with her buttons,' the woman said.

The teenager looked helpless. 'Which one is Sandie?'

'Lizzie, for what I'm paying you, the least you could do is learn to tell them apart,' the woman replied testily. She pointed to one of the septuplets.

So the teenager was some sort of mother's help, Amanda worked out. While they were both occupied with dressing the girls she could creep downstairs, find the kitchen and get something to eat.

Unfortunately, one of the children spotted her. 'Mama, there's Tracey!'

Startled, the woman looked up. For a second she seemed puzzled, then her expression changed to irritation. 'Tracey, why aren't you dressed yet? You're going to be late for the bus and I am *not* driving you to school.'

Fine, Amanda thought, because she had no intention of *going* to school, not as Tracey Devon. She did like the idea of getting out of that horrible nightgown though, and decided to put off scrounging for food until after she'd changed. Besides, maybe by then she'd be out of Tracey's body. She might be eating her very own low-fat, sugar-free muesli in her very own kitchen.

But while she was in this body, she decided she might as well improve the way Tracey dressed for school. Examining the contents of Tracey's wardrobe, however, didn't offer much in the way of anything decent to wear. There was certainly nothing in there that Amanda would want to be seen in. Was the family too poor to buy her clothes? No, that couldn't be it. The house looked OK, and those little clones were wearing cute matching dresses. Once again, it was Tracey's fault – the girl had no taste. Another reason not to feel sorry for her.

Not enough of a reason to get Amanda out of her body though. She opened a drawer and hunted in vain through the piles of plain white knickers for a bra – and then she remembered something else about Tracey. They were in the same PE class and changed in the same locker room. Tracey didn't wear a bra. This was another reason to make fun of her.

With a sigh, Amanda began to search for the least offensive items of clothing. She ended up with a plain denim skirt – no label, of course – and the only T-shirt that didn't have stains in the armpits. The top was far too baggy, but she found a brown belt and cinched it in at her waist. Burrowing through drawers, she couldn't find any make-up – not even a tube of lipgloss – but she did manage to uncover a rubber band, which she used to pull the dirty hair away from Tracey's face and into a high ponytail.

By now she was *starving*. Noise from the room down the hall indicated that everyone was still occupied with the septuplets, so she hurried downstairs and found the kitchen. She spotted a box of muesli bars on the counter and took one. She unwrapped it and managed one bite before mother's-helper Lizzie came in.

'What are you doing? Those are for the girls!'

Amanda chewed and swallowed. 'I'm a girl.'

'You know what I mean.' Lizzie went to the counter and looked into the box. 'Oh no, there are only six left,' she wailed. 'What's your mother going to say?'

Amanda didn't want to know. Suddenly, school didn't seem like such a bad idea.

She recalled seeing a backpack in Tracey's room, and hurried back upstairs. A quick look inside revealed textbooks, so she slung it over her shoulder, ran back downstairs and out the door.

It wasn't hard to spot the bus stop – the school bus was coming up the road and a couple of kids were waiting at the corner. She didn't know any of them, and clearly Tracey didn't either, since none of them acknowledged her arrival. And when the bus stopped and the doors opened just in front of Tracey, they pushed ahead of her to get in. *So rude*. But the bus driver was even ruder – after the boy just in front of her scampered up the steps, the doors closed. As if she wasn't even there!

'Hey!' Amanda yelled, banging on the bus door. 'Open up!'

The driver seemed mildly surprised when she boarded. 'Sorry, I didn't see you,' he muttered.

She was still fuming as she went down the aisle of the bus, which was probably why she didn't see someone's foot sticking out. She tripped over it. Sprawled on the floor, all she could think was – *So this is Tracey's life.* Nobody tried to help her get up, and the guy whose foot was responsible for her fall didn't even bother to apologize. At least no one was laughing – mainly because no one was paying any attention to her. And as she struggled to her feet, she could only pray that she'd be back in her own life very soon. As she made her way to the back of the bus, she decided that the first thing she'd do when she got to school was find herself. Maybe that would provide the jolt to end this transformation.

As soon as she got off the bus, Amanda hurried to her own locker. There she was, fiddling with the combination padlock and talking to Britney, who had the locker next to hers. She'd had the experience before of seeing herself out of someone else's eyes. It was always eerie – but very interesting.

She looked *good*. The striped skirt over the leggings worked – she hadn't been too sure when she'd first contemplated the combination. She wasn't thrilled with the ankle boots though – next time she'd wear ballet flats.

'Amanda?' she said.

She turned, and Amanda-Tracey immediately recognized her own expression – which was exactly the way she would expect to react to any attempt at communication from Tracey Devon. '*What?*'

Amanda-Tracey had no idea how to respond. She'd been hoping that simple face-to-face contact would put her back into her own body.

'Um . . . just wanted to say "hi".'

The other Amanda stared at her in disbelief. Then she turned to Britney, rolled her eyes and said, 'Let's go.'

Amanda-Tracey was disappointed, but she was also relieved. That was definitely genuine Amanda behaviour. As she'd expected, she and Tracey had not swapped bodies — but it was good to have confirmation. She wouldn't have to worry about Tracey saying stupid things, acting nerdy, or otherwise ruining Amanda's reputation.

The warning bell rang, indicating that there were two minutes left before students had to be in their homerooms. It dawned on Amanda that she had no idea where Tracey was supposed to be.

She fumbled through Tracey's backpack and pulled out a lever-arch folder — *that* made sense. Amanda hadn't seen a folder like that since primary school. Everyone in middle school used spiral-bound notebooks, one per class. But luckily, on the inside cover of the folder Tracey had pasted a copy of her timetable. Her classroom was at the other end of the building, on the second floor.

She hurried down the rapidly emptying hallway. Halfway up the stairs the final bell rang, and she sprinted the rest of the way. *Damn!* This was the class where the teachers took the roll and made a big fuss about lateness, and the last thing she wanted to do today was draw attention to herself.

But when she slipped into the classroom, the teacher didn't even glance up. None of the other students took any notice of her either – at least, not until she slid into one of the empty seats. The girl in front of her turned around.

'That's Heather's seat.'

'Sorry,' Amanda said. Then she wanted to kick herself – or better yet, the girl who'd spoken to her. So what if she'd been sitting in Heather's seat? Heather wasn't there. And *why* had she apologized? Was she actually *becoming* Tracey? She looked around. Should she take a chance or ask the girl where Tracey usually sat? No, she couldn't ask – that would be too weird. The girl probably didn't know where Tracey sat anyway, since no one noticed Tracey.

She moved to the other empty seat, and it must have been Tracey's since no one objected. Clearly everyone believed that she was Tracey Devon in Tracey Devon's seat. The mere notion was so horrific she forgot to respond when the teacher called the roll.

'Tracey!' the teacher barked. 'You're actually here, for a change. You might consider answering to your name.' The class giggled knowingly, as if this was some sort of common event.

'Sorry,' Amanda said again, then mentally kicked herself and vowed not to repeat the word for the rest of the day.

After the roll-call came the usual boring announcements over the intercom. Amanda took advantage of the time to consider her situation.

Obviously, this body-transfer experience was different from the previous ones. She'd never spent this long in any other body. On the other hand, the other experiences hadn't been consistent in length – some had lasted seconds, others hours. She'd always come back into herself eventually. She wasn't worried – not yet.

Something else was bothering her though – something she'd never given any thought to before. While she was in another person's body, where was that person? Her memory of being the poor old lady had given her an inkling as to how the other Amanda was functioning – like a robot programmed as Amanda. But where was Tracey?

'Hey, dork, the bell's ringing.'

She looked blankly at the boy passing her desk and realized that homeroom was over. She jumped up and grabbed her backpack. *Get a grip*, she warned herself. *You might have to look like Tracey for a while, but you don't have to be her.*

Tracey's next class was maths, which was not one of Amanda's better subjects. Tracey had the same teacher as Amanda, and they were using the same textbook, but Tracey's class was a couple of days behind Amanda's. Which was kind of cool – for once Amanda knew the answer to the equation that the teacher was writing on the board. When the teacher asked for responses, she raised her hand.

The teacher gazed out over the class. 'Doesn't anyone want to take a stab at this?'

Amanda waved her hand. Then another girl tentatively put her hand up.

'Yes, Jade?'

Amanda lowered her hand. Wow! Was Tracey such a loser that even *teachers* ignored her?

She considered volunteering an answer in Tracey's next class, English, but decided against it. She was better off sticking with her original plan not to call attention to herself. She should just let things run their course, until she could get back into herself and let Tracey pick up where she had left off. It was the least she could do for the poor girl. Oh no! Was a note of pity coming through there?

She checked the timetable in Tracey's folder and saw that her next class was PE. Good – at least she'd be moving around, not just sitting and thinking. But it occurred to her that the gym was just below the classroom she was currently in. It wouldn't take her more than a minute and a half to get there, and there were six minutes to kill between classes. What could she do with them?

In her normal life, she knew exactly what she'd do – go to the closest bathroom and spend the four and a half extra minutes fixing her hair and reapplying lipgloss. She seriously doubted that Tracey visited the bathroom for any reason other than to use the toilet.

On the other hand, lingering in the hall wasn't appealing, and there was no law that kept Tracey out of bathrooms. So when the bell rang, she headed straight for the girls' bathroom across the hall.

She was the first one there. Even though she knew what she'd see when she looked in the mirror, it was still sickening to face Tracey's reflection. No wonder she never stayed long in the bathrooms – who'd want to look at *that* every day? It was just too awful. And even though it wasn't really her, Amanda felt an automatic urge to make some improvement.

Only she had no tools whatsoever. As she'd expected, a search of Tracey's backpack turned up nothing in the way of cosmetics.

The bathroom door opened. In the mirror, Amanda watched as her friends Katie and Emma sauntered in, followed by the Amanda-robot, or whatever she was. They all lined up in front of the mirror, emptied their little make-up bags into the sinks and went to work.

Amanda couldn't take her eyes off herself, and Other-Amanda noticed this. 'What are *you* looking at?'

Wow! If she only knew who she was really speaking to. Amanda held her tongue and said what she assumed Tracey would say in the same situation:

'Nothing.' But when she saw Other-Amanda apply her own Pearls of Rose lipgloss – the very same lipgloss Amanda had bought for herself just last weekend – she spoke impulsively.

'Amanda . . .'

'*What?*'

'Can I borrow your lipgloss?'

Other-Amanda made no attempt to disguise her horrified reaction. 'No!'

Amanda wasn't surprised. If she'd been back in her own body, this was just how she would respond to a request like that from Tracey. After all, she didn't want to get nits, or whatever other kind of disgusting germs someone like Tracey would have.

What did surprise Amanda was the way Other-Amanda's response made her feel. She could actually sense something burning behind her eyes. This was ridiculous – she wasn't Tracey, so why should she care if anyone made fun of her? Even so, Amanda decided to make a fast escape from the bathroom before Tracey's tears made an appearance. She hurried out, down the stairs and into the girls' locker room next to the gym. At least this was one of her own – Amanda's – classes so she knew what would be going on. They were playing volleyball this month. She picked up a clean-but-ugly one-size-fits-all gym uniform and went into the changing room.

All around her, girls were undressing and talking. With her head down, Amanda made her way to an empty locker, hoping to keep a low profile. She particularly wanted to keep away from Other-Amanda. Maybe by now she'd be tired of teasing Tracey about not wearing a bra.

No such luck. As soon as she pulled off the T-shirt, a cry went up.

'Hey, Tracey, have you ever tried this?' Other-Amanda posed with her elbows extended and began to chant while jerking her arms back and forth in an exercise.

'We must, we must, we must increase our bust,
It's better, it's better, it's better for the sweater.'

It was such an old, stale rhyme – how could anyone find it funny any more? But Katie and the others laughed dutifully, and Amanda experienced a strange hot sensation on her face. Ohmigod, was she *blushing*? She'd never blushed before in her life!

The shrill whistle of the PE teacher called them into the gym. Amanda had actually been enjoying PE this month – she was good at volleyball and it brought out her competitive streak. She was always so focused that she never noticed how Tracey had played, but she decided she could safely assume that Tracey was clumsy and she was fairly sure that there was no secret competitive streak hidden behind Tracey's meek demeanour.

Once they were all in the gym, Ms Barnes in her white shorts and shirt blew the whistle again. 'Captains today are Britney and Lorie.' A coin was flipped to see which of the girls would go first, and then team selection began.

If she'd been herself, she'd have been Britney's first choice, Amanda thought sadly. No matter who was captain, she was always the first or second one chosen. But it didn't come as any surprise to find herself still standing between the teams as the selection went on. How humiliating to be the last one left! Again, Amanda had to remind herself that she wasn't herself, that it wasn't really Amanda who had to slink over to Britney's side when there was no one else left to choose.

The game began, and it was a nightmare. Amanda had been half hoping her own personality might override Tracey's natural meekness and physical limitations, but no such luck. Even when she tried her hardest to reach the ball, someone lunged in front of her. Other players pushed her aside like she was an annoying fly that had invaded the gym. Like she didn't belong there at all. A thought hit her: Tracey didn't belong anywhere! She didn't even exist for most people.

Except for you, she told herself grimly. *You* cared. *And look where it got you!*

A ball hitting her in the head brought her back to the game. Not that it did the team any good. It was her turn to serve – and Tracey's best was like Amanda's worst.

The ball hit the net, the game was over, and the team on the other side was cheering.

'Tracey, are you nuts?' Britney shrieked. 'You lost the game, you idiot!'

'Now, now, it's a team sport, we don't blame individuals,' Ms Barnes murmured, but even she was looking at Amanda in despair.

At least Amanda wasn't teased back in the locker room. Her classmates seemed to be satisfied with simply shooting dirty looks at her every time they caught her eye. Or at least, that was how it felt. The only person who didn't look angry was Sarah Miller, but that was no comfort. Sarah was the kind of smiley girl who was always nice to everyone, so as far as Amanda was concerned, she didn't count.

Lunch was next on the timetable – Tracey had the same lunch break as Amanda. But walking into the canteen today was a whole new experience for her. Yesterday it was her kingdom; now, she felt like she was walking into a war zone, with enemies at every table. It was scary.

With her head down, she went to the end of the queue for food. Waiting there, she couldn't resist taking a look at her own table. How strange to see herself sitting there with Katie and all her friends, laughing and talking . . .

'Hey, are you going to move or what?' the guy

behind her demanded.

It was becoming automatic to mumble 'sorry', and she caught up with the queue. Normally she would buy herself only a yoghurt and a salad, but the dish of the day actually looked good and the only happiness she was going to get that day would come from eating. But when she reached the cashier, she realized she'd never checked to see how much money Tracey carried.

Not enough. And so she had to endure more annoyed looks as she backed up and returned the lunch. She ended up with a bar of chocolate and a bag of crisps from the vending machine. She found a seat at an unoccupied table and started to eat. She'd never eaten a lunch alone before. Next time she'd remember to bring a book or a magazine. *But there won't be a next time*, she assured herself. Surely by this time tomorrow she'd be herself again.

With nothing to do but eat her chocolate and crisps, she opened Tracey's binder to see what the rest of the day was going to be like. For the next class, there was no subject like history or English listed – just a room number. 209.

It dawned on her that this could be Tracey's so-called 'gifted' class. And for the first time since that horrible day had begun, she actually felt a little spark of curiosity.

What was that class all about anyway? People called it 'gifted', but there were other classes for brains at Meadowbrook, and they all had names like Advanced Placement English or Advanced Placement Maths.

Maybe it was some kind of special needs class. But no, Tracey was just a nerd, a loser, not someone who needed extra help with learning. So maybe that's what it was – a class for social losers. In the back of her mind, though, Amanda knew that wasn't poss-ible. While the other students would easily classify Tracey as a loser, it wasn't a category Meadow brook Middle School would ever acknowledge. Amanda had a feeling all middle schools were like that. Teachers, principals, guidance counsellors – they never knew what was really going on.

CHAPTER THREE

I T WAS AN ORDINARY CLASSROOM, no different from most of the others in the building. There was a large map on one wall, bookshelves on another, rows of desks and a larger desk at the front of the room, behind which sat a woman.

'Tracey! How nice to *see* you.'

Amanda thought it was an odd greeting from a teacher, especially with the emphasis she put on the word 'see'. Did this have something to do with being 'seen and not heard'? Was Tracey actually noisy in this class? That was hard to believe.

Since she had no idea what the teacher's name was, she responded with, 'Nice to see you too,' and then turned to see who else was there. The bell hadn't yet rung, and there were only two other students seated in the room. One was a small, round-faced boy with unfashionably short hair and a solemn expression. He looked very young – a sixth grader maybe? In any case, she'd never seen him before.

But the other face was definitely familiar. It was funny in a way, because she'd been thinking about her just the other day – Jenna Kelley. Ordinarily Amanda wouldn't know the names of seventh graders, but Jenna was famous – or maybe *infamous* was the right word. And it wasn't just because she always wore black and rimmed her eyes with kohl.

There were stories about Jenna Kelley, and they weren't just rumours. She'd moved to Meadowbrook just after the beginning of the school year, and not from another middle school, but from some sort of jail for juvenile delinquents. Amanda had no idea why Jenna had been in the place, but she had to believe it was something bigger than shoplifting. Jenna was scary-looking, like someone who carried a switchblade and wouldn't mind cutting the face of anyone who annoyed her. What was impossible to believe was the notion that Jenna might be 'gifted', unless gifted was a polite term for something else. Like criminally insane?

But that notion vanished with the next arrival.

'Ken!' Amanda exclaimed.

Ken Preston looked at her blankly. 'Yeah?'

Then she remembered that Ken wasn't responding to Amanda Beeson, the girl he'd kissed under the water at Sophie's pool party last August. He was addressing Tracey Devon, who would never have the nerve to speak to a hot guy like him, and he was now looking quizzically at Amanda-Tracey, wondering what she wanted.

'Uh, nothing,' Amanda mumbled. 'Sorry.' For once, she uttered that word intentionally. She had just decided that in this class, she actually needed to behave like Tracey. The last thing in the world she wanted was for anyone here – meaning Ken – to find out who she really was. If Ken knew what was going on, she had an awful feeling he would never be able to look at her again without seeing Tracey's face.

'Hello, Ken,' the teacher said as he ambled to a seat.

'Hi, Madame,' Ken replied.

Madame. That was interesting, Amanda thought. Maybe she was a French teacher at Meadowbrook. That would explain why Amanda had never seen her before.

The next person to join the class was another surprise – Sarah Miller, the super-sweet girl who was in her PE class. Why was *she* here? Because she was too good to be true? Was *that* a gift?

But Amanda was more intrigued by the fact that Ken Preston, too cute and so *not* a criminal or a smiley type, was here. He was super-popular, and he'd been the star of the school soccer team till he had that awful accident the previous month. And even though he wasn't on the team any more, he was still considered one of the coolest guys at Meadowbrook. So why was *he* in this class? She didn't think being cool counted as being gifted. If that had been the case, she, the real Amanda, would have been there.

The next student to enter was a young-looking girl with a glazed expression. The teacher greeted her as 'Emily', and she took the seat next to Amanda.

Then in came a boy who Amanda had noticed before because he was the only student at Meadowbrook in a wheelchair. He was followed by yet another boy, and this time Amanda drew in her breath sharply.

She recognized him immediately even though she hadn't seen him in ages – Martin Cooper, who used to live across the street. The boy whose body she'd briefly occupied so long ago. He must be in the sixth grade now . . . but he still looked exactly the way he'd looked back when he was the most picked-on boy in the neighbourhood.

Maybe Tracey got picked on a lot and that was a reason to be in this class. On the other hand, no one would ever pick on Jenna – not if they wanted to live. And who would pick on Ken Preston?

The bell rang, and Amanda counted eight students in the class. The average class at Meadowbrook had between twenty and thirty students. This was getting more and more mysterious.

Madame rose from her chair and came around to the front of the desk. She was a petite, dark-haired woman with bright, dark eyes and a friendly smile.

'Charles, would you like to begin your report?'

'No,' replied the boy in the wheelchair.

Amanda was slightly taken aback. No one ever wanted to give reports, but no one ever actually said no. You made excuses – you claimed you'd left your notes at home, you pretended to have laryngitis – but you didn't just say no.

Madame didn't seem surprised, just disappointed. 'This is your day to report, Charles.'

'I'm not ready,' Charles said flatly.

'The assignment was set more than a week ago – you've had plenty of time to prepare.'

'I've been busy.'

Jenna spoke suddenly. 'Liar.'

Charles turned his head. 'What did you say?'

'You're lying,' Jenna said. 'You haven't been busy. You just don't *want* to give your report.'

'How would *you* know?' Charles snapped. Laughter swept across the classroom and Charles reddened.

Amanda didn't get it, and figured this had to be some sort of in-joke. She could see that Madame didn't appreciate it.

'That was an inappropriate remark, Jenna. You have to respect the privacy of Charles's thoughts.'

Jenna shrugged. 'It just slipped out.'

Madame looked at her pointedly. 'We've talked about this before, Jenna. You have to learn to control your gift. You all do. Now, Charles, you do need to give us a report today. If you haven't prepared anything, you still have to respond to the assignment. You'll just need to speak off the cuff.'

Charles's lips were set in a tight line and he stared at his desk. Amanda wondered why Madame didn't do what any other teacher would do in this kind of situation – send him to the principal's office, give him a zero for the assignment, that sort of thing. This teacher didn't even seem upset.

She continued to speak calmly. 'Would someone like to remind Charles of this week's assignment?'

The spacey-looking girl spoke. '"Give an example of how you misused your gift during the past month." Like, when I knew it was going to rain on Saturday, so I told Heather not to have a picnic, and—'

Madame cut her off. 'That's enough, Emily. This

is Charles's turn. Charles?'

Amanda watched him with some alarm. The boy in the wheelchair was getting awfully pale, like he was about to be sick or something. She was glad *she* wasn't sitting next to him. Poor Ken . . . Was he about to get puked on?

Ken spoke to him. 'Look, man, you've got to confront your problem, y'know?'

'Not "problem", Ken,' Madame corrected him. 'We use the word "gift".'

Charles glared at Ken. 'What do *you* know about my life? You're a jock!'

'Not any more,' Ken said.

'Well, that's your choice. You're not stuck in a wheelchair!'

So that's it, Amanda thought. She'd seen something like this on TV. This was some sort of group therapy for kids with personal problems, hang-ups. Emotional stuff. No wonder people were so secretive about it. You wouldn't want your classmates to know you were some kind of basket case.

It all made sense to her now, except for one thing. Why did the teacher refer to their problems as 'gifts'?

Ken continued. 'Hey, all I'm saying is that you shouldn't put off talking about your prob— your *gift*. I mean, the rest of us gave our reports – why can't you?'

Now Charles's eyes were blazing. 'Because I don't feel like it, OK?' His voice was rising. 'And you're really annoying me, you know? Just because I'm in a wheelchair doesn't mean you can push me around! So mind your own stupid business, you – you –' He was almost shrieking now, which was creepy, but what was even creepier was the way little Martin suddenly dropped to the floor and crawled under his desk . . . just before several books came flying off the bookshelf.

Everyone ducked as the books soared by. Amanda was so startled she didn't move fast enough, and a book clipped her ear. 'Ow!'

'Sarah, make him stop!' someone yelled. *But how could Sarah do anything about it?* Amanda wondered. She was sitting on the other side of the room. In any case, Madame was able to put an end to the chaos.

'Charles!' the teacher yelled sharply. 'Stop it right now! Control yourself!'

The flight of the books continued, but they were moving more slowly, and then began dropping to the floor.

Madame now wore a very stern expression. 'That was completely unnecessary, Charles. I'm going to give you five demerits.' The small potted plant on her desk began to rise.

'*Charles!*' she said in a warning tone. The plant came back down.

Amanda, in a state of shock, was still clutching her ear. Madame noticed this. 'Tracey, are you all right?'

Amanda took her hand away and looked at it. There was no blood. 'I – uh – yes.'

The teacher went behind her desk, opened a notebook and began jotting something down. Amanda turned to Emily. 'What was all *that* about?'

Emily's vacant eyes focused slightly. 'Oh come on, Tracey. You don't have to be able to see into the future to know what Charles does when he gets angry.'

'Madame?'

'Yes, Jenna?'

'Martin has to go to the bathroom.'

There were a couple of snickers, and Martin cowered in his seat.

Madame looked pained. 'Jenna, Martin is fully capable of asking to be excused himself.'

Jenna's innocent expression didn't mask a nasty twinkle in her eyes. 'But you know how shy he is, Madame. And I swear, he's just about to wet himself.'

'Am not!' Martin squeaked, but he looked very nervous.

'Martin, you may go to the bathroom,' Madame said.

As Martin scurried out the door, Amanda turned to Emily. 'But how did Jenna know . . .'

'Jenna, I don't want to have to say this again,' Madame declared. 'You're behaving very badly. Just because you have the ability to read other people's minds doesn't mean you have the *right* to do this. Not to mention the fact that you know what Martin does when he feels picked on.'

Jenna slumped back in her seat. 'Yeah, OK.'

Madame shook her head wearily. 'Charles has already created a mess in the room; we certainly don't need Martin to hurt anyone. Now, class, for the rest of the time we're going to work on breathing exercises.'

There was a loud groan from the students – except Sarah, of course. Amanda wondered if she ever complained about anything.

Madame frowned.

'These exercises are essential for establishing control. Now, let's go over the five basic steps.' She turned and began writing on the blackboard. 'Step one: don't breathe through your nose. Concentrate on expanding your lungs . . .'

Amanda was neither listening nor looking at the blackboard. Her head was spinning so fast she felt dizzy. What was going on here? Charles making things move; Jenna reading minds; wimpy little Martin Cooper . . . hurting someone? How? Who *were* these people?

This was a fantasy – it couldn't be happening. People like this, people with strange powers – they belonged in movies like *X-Men*, or Japanese cartoons. How could she have ever guessed there were people like this at Meadowbrook Middle School? Forget about Meadowbrook – these people weren't supposed to exist anywhere in the real world.

Psychos. Freaks. Monsters. She didn't know what to call them. Ken was one of them . . . and Sarah Miller. What kind of powers did *they* have?

And ohmigod! What kind of psycho-freak was Tracey Devon?

Chapter Four

JENNA WAS HAVING TROUBLE keeping her eyes open. As she went through the motions of Madame's breathing exercises, she used every intake of breath as an excuse to yawn. This meant that she always breathed out a second or two after the others in the class, which resulted in a frown aimed in her direction from Madame. Not that she cared what Madame thought of her – but there was something about the teacher that always made her cringe a little. It was almost as if Madame could see what was going on in Jenna's head, which was ridiculous, of course. Only Jenna could see what was going on in the minds of others. Strangely enough, however, she could never completely penetrate Madame's head. Not that she ever really wanted to. After all, what sort of interesting thoughts could a *teacher* be having?

Madame took her attention away from Jenna as she offered a sullen Charles some advice about the rhythm of his breathing. Jenna took advantage of this and closed her eyes. She could fall asleep so easily ...

There were two reasons for this. She'd been up very late the night before. She wasn't exactly sure what time she'd drifted off, but she thought she could see the first rays of dawn from her bedroom window. So she hadn't had much sleep, and that alone justified her yawning.

The other reason was the fact that she was bored, but it wasn't an unusual state of mind for her, especially here. Her classes were boring, her teachers were boring, and what was the point in being there anyway? She just didn't care what went on at school.

This class was the worst. It was too small and she couldn't hide. In other classes she sat at the back, where the teacher wouldn't notice her. There she could tune out and amuse herself by listening to her classmates' thoughts. They were never particularly amusing or even mildly interesting – other people's daydreams could be as dull as dirt. But in this class she couldn't even do that. Madame knew her gift, and she was always watching Jenna's face for telltale signs of mental eavesdropping.

Of course there were times when Madame was occupied with other students, like right now, and Jenna could concentrate on reading the minds of others. But these so-called gifted kids weren't any more entertaining than her usual classmates. Charles, for example, thought only about stuff like what he was going to demand for dinner that evening or what he'd make everyone watch on TV. It seemed to her like he totally ruled the roost at home.

Madame was helping Ken breathe now, so Jenna turned her attention to Emily. When she'd first learned about Emily's gift, Jenna had hoped to find something interesting in her head. But Emily was a total space cadet – she had no control over her gift at all. At this moment, all Jenna could see was a vague image of a raging forest fire. Somewhere, at some time in the near or distant future, a load of trees would burn. Maybe. It was impossible to tell whether Emily was having visions or simply daydreaming.

She focused on Martin's thoughts, but she knew there would be nothing remarkable there. Martin's head was packed with memories of all the times he had felt like a victim. The only moments when it could be intriguing to read Martin occurred when he was angry. Then Jenna could see a brilliant display of sparkling lights in lots of different colours, something like fireworks.

Sarah's thoughts were pretty boring. You'd think that a girl who could control other people might have some interesting ideas in her head, but Sarah was so *not* into using her power that she refused to even think about it. It was like she was in some sort of zen state all the time.

She didn't bother to try Carter, the youngest student in the group. She knew there would be nothing in his head. Sometimes she wondered how the strange boy could walk and eat and put on his clothes when it seemed to her he didn't even have a brain.

Tracey was almost worse than nothing. Her thoughts were formless, just a big thick black cloud of misery. Whatever bits and pieces Jenna could decipher were usually too depressing to read . . .

She frowned. Something unfamiliar was coming

from Tracey's mind. There was a light . . . Jenna stared at her and tried to concentrate, to see into the light. But before she could make any sense out of it, someone else's thoughts broke in.

She murdered me, and now she's getting away with it! She has to be arrested! Help me! Tell the police!

There was only one head that could produce a thought like this.

'Hey, Ken,' she whispered. 'Someone's calling you.'

Madame heard her. 'Jenna! What did I tell you about eavesdropping?'

'It's OK, Madame,' Ken said wearily. 'You can't really blame her. This guy is so *loud*.'

'No kidding,' Jenna said. 'I didn't even have to *try* to listen.'

'Would you like to share this problem with us, Ken?' Madame asked.

Ken sighed. 'He pops in about once a week or so, and he's really annoying me. Supposedly he was killed in an accident – he fell down some stairs and hit his head. But he claims his wife murdered him, and he wants me to call the police.'

'So why don't you just do what he says?' Jenna

suggested. 'Tell the cops and then he'll stop bugging you.'

Ken shook his head. 'I don't want to get involved. Besides, what am I going to say? "Hello, Mister Policeman. A dead man asked me to give you a message"? They'll think I'm nuts!'

'Class, we've talked about this kind of problem before,' Madame said. 'What do we do when our gifts intrude on our lives? Martin?'

The scrawny little wimp murmured the standard response. 'We're supposed to ignore them.'

'Exactly. And if they persist? Charles?'

The boy slumped in the wheelchair spoke. 'I dunno.'

Madame looked at him reprovingly. 'Nonsense, Charles! You know what you're supposed to do, even if you don't always do it.'

Charles mumbled something.

'What did you say, Charles? We can't hear you.'

'You push them away!' Charles snapped. The flower vase on Madame's desk quivered.

Madame glared at him. 'Charles!'

The vase was still.

'Thank you, Charles. Yes, you're correct. We concentrate on forcibly pushing the gift away.'

'I'm trying to lose him, Madame,' Ken declared, 'but this guy's really persistent.'

Madame nodded sympathetically and addressed the group. 'Class, Ken needs our help. Let's try to come up with some ideas for him.'

Jenna hadn't meant for the groan to escape her lips quite so loudly. Now *everyone* was glaring at her.

'Wow, Jenna! Why do you have to be such a—' Ken caught himself. 'Well, you know what I mean.'

'We're all in this together, Jenna,' Emily added softly. 'We have to care about each other.'

Madame joined in. 'We need each other's support.'

Not me, Jenna thought, but she managed to keep this to herself and tried to stop her expression from showing what she was thinking. *What a bunch of losers! I don't want to hear any of their opinions about anything.*

Happily, the bell rang just then, so she didn't have to.

'We'll continue this discussion tomorrow,'

Madame said. 'And your assignment for tomorrow's class is to report on a moment when you successfully controlled your gift.'

As Jenna moved to the door she passed Tracey, and once again she got a glimpse of something unusual from her. But when their eyes met, Tracey let out a frightened little squeak and scampered away.

Jenna didn't really care. Even if there was something new going on in Tracey's dull little head, what difference would it make? They were all nerds, these so-called gifted kids, each of them living a sad, pathetic, boring life.

Not like *her* life . . .

CHAPTER FIVE

AMANDA WAS WATCHING THE clock. For a while now she'd wondered if maybe, when the final bell rang, her nightmare would be over. She had no real reason to believe this would happen. Her transformation hadn't begun with the first bell at school, so why would it end with the last bell?

Still, she harboured a hope. After all, that last bell held a lot of meaning, not only for her but for all students at Meadowbrook, and maybe for the teachers too. It was a big deal: it meant the end of the school day, dismissal, escape, freedom from authority. So maybe, just maybe, that bell would signify her own freedom, her escape from the prison of Tracey's wretched body.

But at 3.45 that afternoon, Amanda Beeson

walked out of Meadowbrook Middle School in the same condition she'd entered it that morning: as Tracey Devon. So Amanda revised her expectations. She'd woken that morning as Tracey, and she wouldn't be herself till she woke up the following morning. Somehow she'd have to get through the rest of the day and the night as the number-one nerd of the universe. She planned to go to bed *very* early.

Meanwhile, there was no place for her to go other than Tracey's home. So she went over to the place where the kids who took the bus were supposed to wait for it. This time she recognized one of the travellers – a boy who had been in Tracey's social-studies class. Amanda couldn't remember his name, but she thought he was kind of cute, so she decided to strike up a conversation.

'Hi.'

The boy didn't even turn in her direction.

She raised her voice. '*Hi.*'

He glanced at her. 'What?'

Clearly, this boy had no conversation skills. So Amanda plunged in with a safe, sure-fire remark that was bound to get him to talk. 'Can you *believe* how much homework Ms Dailey gave us?'

She waited for the expected response – wholehearted agreement, a grumble, something like that. Instead the boy backed away and started up a conversation with another girl.

Well, what did she expect? They thought she was Tracey Devon. If only those boys knew who was really standing right by them, who was actually speaking to them, they'd be thrilled; they'd be all over themselves, showing off, trying to impress her. That knowledge gave her a tiny bit of satisfaction, but she still felt down.

The bus arrived, and Amanda saw that the driver was the same man who had picked them up that morning. This time she made sure she was at the front of the group so she could get on first and grab a front seat. She didn't want to have to go down the aisle, where someone could trip her.

But once again, when the bus doors opened, she was shoved out of the way and pushed to the back of the group. And again the bus doors closed in her face.

She moved to bang on the doors, but this time she

got there too late. Someone at a window saw her, but he didn't tell the driver. He just grinned and stuck out his tongue as the bus took off.

Amanda stood there, fuming. Was the man blind or something? What was he doing driving a school bus? Maybe she should tell her mother – no, Tracey's mother – to make a complaint to the school.

And now she'd have to walk to Tracey's home. She tried to recall the route the bus had taken that morning, and she thought she had a pretty good idea how to get there. But she was unfamiliar with the neighbourhood, so of course she made a couple of wrong turns and had to backtrack twice. A trip that took ten minutes by bus took her over an hour.

As she turned on to Tracey's street, she imagined the scene that would take place when she arrived at the house. Tracey's mother would be worried. When she, Amanda, came home later than expected, she sometimes found her mother on the verge of tears, ready to call the police and report her as a missing person.

Her friends' parents were like this too, reacting strongly, but sometimes in different ways. She remembered Britney's mother yelling at her, and Katie could even get grounded if she came home late three times in a row.

Maybe Tracey's mother wouldn't be too angry if Amanda pointed out that it wasn't her fault, that the driver just didn't see her. In any case, she wasn't looking forward to the confrontation. A few more minutes wouldn't make any difference, so she walked slowly and used the time to examine Tracey's neighbourhood.

Amanda lived in an older part of town, where the houses were huge and surrounded by big leafy trees. This was one of the new neighbourhoods, with modern-looking houses – nice, though not as grand as the ones in Amanda's area. It dawned on her that this wasn't where Tracey had lived when they were in primary school together.

How did she know this? Maybe it was being in Tracey's body that made her remember something she'd long ago forgotten – going to Tracey's seventh birthday party, when they'd been in the same second-grade class. The Devon family were only three people then, Tracey and her two parents, and they'd lived in a two-bedroom apartment in a leafy development. They must have moved to this neighbourhood when the Devon Seven were born and they'd needed more space.

It was hard to believe that she, Amanda Beeson, the Queen of Meadowbrook Middle School, had ever really gone to a party for Meadowbrook's number-one nobody, Tracey Devon. Amanda couldn't remember if her mother had forced her to go. What she did remember was an ordinary birthday party, with the usual games, a cake and candles . . . But now that she thought about it, she had the same notion she'd had earlier – that Tracey had been an ordinary, normal person back then. Not one of her friends, but not a hopeless weirdo either. Briefly, she wondered what could have happened to her between then and now. An accident? Some kind of brain injury?

She was at Tracey's door now, and she took a deep breath. Then she turned the handle, walked in, and called out, 'I'm home!' That was what Amanda always did when she arrived at her house every day after school.

But apparently, this was not what Tracey did. Mrs Devon shot out of a room upstairs and appeared on the landing that overlooked the living room.

'Quiet!' she hissed. 'The girls are napping!' Then she went back into whatever room she'd come out of.

'Sorry,' Amanda murmured to no one, and ambled into the kitchen. Back at her own home, her mother would now make her a little after-school snack or, if she was out, the snack would be waiting for her on the counter. She brightened when she spotted a box of cupcakes on the Devon kitchen counter, but before she could help herself to one, the teenage mother's help came into the room.

'Don't touch those – they're for the girls!'

'What's for me?' Amanda asked, but Lizzie had already hurried out of the room.

Amanda spotted a basket of apples on the table. She did a quick count, saw that there were more than seven, and took one. Biting into it, she went back out into the living room and looked around.

Some framed photos hung in a cluster on the wall, and while she ate her apple she went over to examine them more closely. There was a traditional bride-and-groom picture of a woman she could identify as a younger version of Tracey's nasty mother, and she assumed the man in the picture was her father. Then there was another photo of the couple, older, beaming proudly as they stood beside an oversize cradle packed with seven tiny babies. The rest of the pictures were group photos of the septuplets on their birthdays, and individual shots of each septuplet at each age. One would have been enough, Amanda thought – the little girls looked exactly alike.

And where was Tracey? She finally located another picture, which seemed to be a framed version of the previous year's family Christmas card. There they were, the seven little smiling Devon girls standing in a row in front of their parents. Looking more closely, Amanda was able to make out Tracey, half hidden behind the Christmas tree. Funny – it was a good shot of all the others, but Tracey looked sort of fuzzy.

It was clear to her that Tracey wasn't the star of this family or even a featured player. There was absolutely nothing else about her in the room – nothing like the kind of stuff Amanda could see in her own home and the homes of her friends. There were no awards or citations or blue ribbons, no medals, no statuettes of gymnasts or figure skaters.

Despite her previous total lack of interest in Tracey Devon, Amanda found that she was becoming curious about the girl. She went upstairs to the room she'd woken up in that morning. Surely here she'd be able to find some clues about Tracey's life.

She remembered noting in the morning that there was nothing on the walls, and that was strange. Most girls she knew had posters – rock stars, horses, a popular TV series, stuff like that. Tracey's walls were bare. Amanda looked on shelves, in drawers, even under the bed, but after twenty minutes of searching she was completely mystified. She'd found nothing that gave her the tiniest hint as to what Tracey Devon was all about. There were no books, no CDs, no magazines.

But ultimately, her search paid off. At the back of Tracey's cupboard, under the laundry basket, she discovered a pink notebook. Scrawled on the cover, in childish handwriting, were the words: *Tracey Devon, My Diary. Private, Keep Out!*

Amanda ignored the warning. Settling down on Tracey's bed, she opened the book to the first page.

'Dear Diary, I'm seven years old today! I had a party with all my friends. We had chocolate cake with pink roses on it. I got lots of presents. But Mommy and Daddy say I have to wait a whole month for my biggest present. They are going to give me real live babies! I hope they are all girls. Boys are icky.'

She turned to the next page.

'Dear Diary, I got 100 on my spelling test! Mommy took me out for ice cream. Daddy says I'm the smartest girl in the world.'

And on the next page:

'Dear Diary, I went to swimming class today. We are learning how to dive. It's fun.'

Tracey definitely sounded like an ordinary person in her diary, Amanda thought. This was all so normal, it was boring. She wasn't going to learn anything interesting here. She closed the notebook and tossed it on the floor.

Of course, it didn't really matter. Amanda was completely confident that she'd be out of this dismal cell in the morning, so it wasn't as if she really needed to know the girl well. She paused in front of the mirror and forced herself to take another look at Tracey.

This mirror can't be very clean, she thought. The reflected image seemed blurry to her. Which was just as well, she supposed, taking into consideration how awful Tracey looked.

Suddenly an idea hit her, and she almost smiled for the first time that day. She'd thought of a way to occupy her time and actually do a good deed while she was here. (Not that good deeds were a habit with her, but she figured she might be rewarded for it by positive forces and get out of Tracey's body even sooner.)

There was something very significant that she could do for this poor girl – she could make Tracey look better! Now, this day, while she had control of Tracey's body, she could get the girl a decent haircut, some cool clothes, lipgloss and maybe some blusher to brighten her drab complexion. She'd be helping herself too – if Tracey wasn't so pathetic, Amanda wouldn't have to worry about feeling sorry for her and finding herself in this situation again.

She already knew that Tracey wasn't carrying any money, and she hadn't found any in her search of the room, but from the look of the house she could see that the family wasn't poor. She headed off to look for Tracey's mother.

She found her in a room she hadn't seen earlier – a cosy den with a TV. Mrs Devon was sitting on the sofa, talking on the phone as she leafed through what looked like a clothing catalogue.

'Lila, these things are so cute!' she squealed. 'My girls are going to look adorable this winter. I'm going to order the little pink matching hats and mittens . . .'

If this had been her own home Amanda would just have interrupted, but here she waited for a pause in the conversation, tapping her foot impatiently, so she could break in. She had to decide how she was going to address the woman anyway.

She had no idea what Tracey called her. Mom? Mommy? Mother?

'Go ahead and answer the door, Lila – I'll hold on,' Mrs Devon said, and Amanda took a chance. 'Mom?'

There was no response as the woman turned the page of the catalogue.

'Mommy?' she said. 'Mother?'

The woman lifted her head and looked at Amanda blankly. 'Did you say something?'

'I was just wondering – could we go shopping?'

'What? Go where?'

'Shopping. Like, we could go to the mall.'

She responded as if Amanda had suggested a trip to the moon. 'The *mall*?'

'Yeah. Not the big one on the highway – the other one, across from Meadowbrook . . .' Her voice trailed off as Mrs Devon's expression went from puzzlement to disbelief to something very close to anger.

'Are you insane? Have you lost your mind? Don't be ridiculous! I don't have time to go shopping. I have seven children upstairs!'

It was on the tip of Amanda's tongue to say, 'You have *eight* children,' but Mrs Devon's friend had returned to the phone.

'Yes, Lila, I'm here. I just have to run to the drug-store to pick up the girls' vitamins. Of course we could have a coffee. I've got the mother's help here and the girls are napping. OK, see you in ten minutes.'

Amanda was stunned. As Mrs Devon hung up the phone, she glared at the woman. 'You've got time to meet your friend, but you can't take me shopping?'

But Mrs Devon walked right past her like she wasn't even there.

CHAPTER SIX

J ENNA DIDN'T PARTICULARLY LIKE any day of the week, but she really hated Wednesdays. Every Wednesday, after her last class, she had to visit the school counsellor.

This was a requirement that the judge had imposed when Jenna was released after a month in the reform school. If she skipped the meetings, the counsellor would report her to the judge, and the judge could send her back to that place, where many of the kids were even tougher than she was.

She rapped on Mr Gonzalez's door and waited for his cheerful, booming voice to call, 'Come in!' As usual, he was sitting *on* his desk instead of behind it.

'Hiya, Jenna!' he said with a smile.

It was very hard for her not to smile back. She actually kind of sort of liked Mr Gonzalez, but she couldn't let him know that. So she just muttered something that sounded like an unenthusiastic greeting and took her usual seat.

'How are you doing?' Mr Gonzalez asked.

'OK,' Jenna mumbled.

'Just OK? Come on, give me something more interesting than that. Fabulous, excited, miserable, angry – anything's better than just OK.'

'I'm a little tired,' she admitted.

'Why is that? Are you having trouble sleeping?'

It was the perfect opportunity to go into her pose. 'Nah, I was out late last night. Hanging with my crew.' She liked the word *crew*. She'd picked it up from a TV show and it sounded so much cooler than *gang*.

Mr Gonzalez frowned slightly. 'Jenna, you know you have a curfew. You're supposed to be back at home by ten o'clock at night.'

She'd forgotten that, and it was another requirement handed down by the judge. Hastily, she amended her statement. 'Well, I wasn't exactly *out*. The crew were at my place.'

'Did your mother approve of that?'

'Um, she didn't know. She was out.'

'I see,' Mr Gonzalez said. He picked up a pen and jotted something down in the notebook that was open on his desk. Jenna stiffened.

'She wasn't out all night or anything like that,' she said. 'She was home before eleven.'

'And she let your friends stay?'

Jenna thought quickly. 'Uh, she didn't know they were there. They were in my room and the door was closed.'

Was he buying it? She searched his mind and saw that it was cloudy with doubts. She had to move the conversation along, so she improvised. 'Um, one of the guys in my crew, he, uh, offered me some drugs, but I said no. And I made him leave,' she added.

'Good,' he said. 'Were you tempted to take the drugs?'

'Oh no,' Jenna assured him. 'I never touch drugs any more.' Actually, she'd never even tried drugs, but it was one of the reasons she'd been arrested six months ago – she'd been with people who were high. She didn't mind people thinking she'd been into drugs at one time. It was good for her bad reputation.

To her relief, the topic of conversation shifted to classes and grades – much safer subjects for Jenna. Not that she was doing brilliantly, but she'd managed to keep her performance at slightly below average, doing just well enough to keep her from getting reported to anyone official. She didn't want to do any better than that – it wouldn't be good for her image.

Thank goodness Mr Gonzalez couldn't read *her* mind. While she pretended to listen as he talked about how bright she was, and how she could do so much better and maybe get a scholarship to a university some day, her thoughts hovered around the real events of the night before.

She hadn't been with her 'crew'. She really didn't have a crew, unless she counted the sad bunch she sometimes lingered with around the train station, when anything was better than being in her own house.

She'd actually been at home the evening before, with plans to watch a couple of things on TV and then go to bed. But her mother had arrived home with friends, they'd put on some music and started dancing, and there was no way Jenna could sleep through that in a tiny apartment. They must have been drinking too, because her mother was sick and Jenna had had to clean it up.

So it really hadn't been her fault that she hadn't got much sleep the night before, but she couldn't tell Mr Gonzalez the real story. If the judge knew how her mother was behaving, that just might be another reason to send Jenna away.

It was funny, in a way. She thought the others in her so-called 'gifted' class had crummy lives – lives completely unlike hers. Only every now and then she had to admit that her life sucked too.

But there was no way she'd ever let anyone else know that.

Amanda had nothing to do. She'd finished Tracey's homework and she'd even made Tracey's bed (which was something she rarely did with her own bed at home). She wondered if there were chores Tracey was supposed to do, like set the table for dinner. She supposed she could ask Lizzie, the mother's help. On the other hand she didn't particularly feel like talking to the teenager, who was always scolding her for eating something that belonged to the septuplets.

She picked up Tracey's diary from the floor. This time she opened it to the middle. From the date, she could see it was two years after the last entry she'd read. Tracey would have been nine. There was only one line on the page.

'Dear Diary, Sometimes I hate them.'

Hate who? The kids at school? So why didn't Tracey do anything about it? Frustrated, Amanda tossed the notebook back on the floor.

Maybe there was something on TV. She went back downstairs to the little room where she'd spotted a television set. But the Devon Seven were up from their naps and they were now gathered in that room with Lizzie, sitting on the rug and watching some dumb kiddie show.

She stood in the doorway for a moment, and one of the seven actually looked at her. 'Hi, Tracey.'

She had a feeling it was the same one who had noticed her that morning, but she couldn't be sure. And what did it matter – they weren't *her* sisters. So she didn't even bother to respond to the kid.

On the bookshelf, she saw something that looked

like a photo album. She picked it up and sat down on the little sofa with it.

The first few pages contained very old photos, black and white, of people in old-fashioned clothes. She thought they might be Tracey's grandparents or great-grandparents. In any case, they weren't very interesting. She kept turning pages until she spotted someone she recognized – Mrs Devon as a young teenager, maybe thirteen. At least, she assumed it was Mrs Devon, because she looked a little like Tracey. Or the way Tracey might look if she wasn't so awful.

The girl in the photo was thin, but Amanda would describe her as slender, not scrawny. And she was blonde, but her hair was chin-length, short and bouncy, not hanging in flat, stringy clumps. She had pale blue eyes like Tracey's, but they were bright, not watery. There were freckles on her face too, but they looked cute. And she had the same thin lips, but they were rosy pink and stretched into a smile. Amanda couldn't remember ever seeing Tracey smile. Maybe at that seventh birthday party . . .

Young Mrs Devon was wearing some cute clothes too. Even though the photo had to be, like, thirty years old, the miniskirt she wore would even look OK today, though Amanda wasn't so sure about the white boots.

She turned the page. There were more photos of Mrs Devon, becoming more and more recognizable as she grew older. There was a copy of the same wedding picture she'd seen on the wall in the living room. And a couple of pages later, the same couple stood in a similar pose, but this time Mrs Devon was holding a baby.

The baby must be Tracey, Amanda realized. She examined the picture closely. Well, Tracey had obviously been born normal – she looked like any other baby, cute and plump, and her parents looked very happy to have her.

There were more pictures of Tracey on the following pages – Tracey in adorable little-girl ruffled and smocked dresses, Tracey wearing a swimsuit and sitting in a paddling pool, Tracey on her father's shoulders. In almost every photo, Tracey was smiling or laughing, her eyes crinkling. On the next page, Amanda saw a first-day-of-school photo – there was one almost exactly like it in the Beeson family album, and it seemed to Amanda that little Tracey was carrying the same pink Hello Kitty backpack that little Amanda carried in her picture.

Then she came to a photo that made her gasp. It was Tracey's seventh birthday party, with all the guests at the table and Tracey in the centre. Amanda saw herself, and she recognized her friends Sophie and Nina, who had been in the same second-grade class with Tracey too. That wasn't such a shock – at that age, all the girls in a class were invited to one another's birthday parties. What really blew her mind was the way she and Sophie had their arms around Tracey, as if they were actually friends! It seemed completely natural too, since Tracey looked just as cute and happy as the rest of them.

Mrs Devon was in the picture too, standing behind Tracey, and it was clear from the size of her that she was hugely pregnant. That was the year the Devon Seven were born, Amanda remembered.

On the next page there were no pictures of Tracey at all.

Practically every picture in the rest of the album portrayed the septuplets – together, individually, sometimes with the parents. Occasionally there was a glimpse of Tracey, but her image was always half hidden or blurred.

From the kitchen came the sound of pots and pans clattering, and Amanda guessed that Mrs Devon must have come home. A moment later, she heard the woman's voice.

'Lizzie! Could you help me with dinner?'

Lizzie left the room, and Amanda wondered if she should help too. But Mrs Devon hadn't called for her . . .

'Tracey?'

This time Amanda was almost sure the septuplet who spoke was the same one who had spoken to her that morning. 'What?'

'Can you read us a story?'

Now seven little faces were looking at her expectantly. Amanda had to admit they were pretty cute. But before she could respond to the request, she heard the front door open, and a man's voice called out, 'I'm home!'

The Devon Seven jumped up and ran out of the room. Cries of 'Daddy! Daddy!' filled the air. Slowly

Amanda got up and went into the hallway, where she could see what was happening in the living room.

'Here are my girls!' Mr Devon sang out as he made silly efforts to gather all the children in his arms. 'Hello, Sandie, Mandie, Randie, Kandie, Brandie, Tandie and Vandie!' The septuplets were giggling like crazy as, one at a time, he lifted the girls in the air. He didn't seem to see Tracey in the hallway, and he didn't ask for her either.

That was when Amanda knew who Tracey sometimes hated. Her little sisters. Once they were born Tracey was pushed aside, and nobody paid any attention to her.

'Dinner's on the table,' Mrs Devon called. Her husband and the Devon Seven took off in that direction.

Amanda followed, but she wondered as she went if there'd even be a place set for Tracey.

CHAPTER SEVEN

AMANDA WAS THE FIRST to arrive in the gifted class the next day, and she'd hurried there on purpose. This was probably the only place at Meadowbrook where she would get any attention – *positive* attention, that is. In PE, the girl with her face claimed to have seen an insect crawl out of Tracey's hair. Which wasn't true, of course. But Amanda-Tracey hadn't been able to laugh or contradict her. It was strange – her other self was getting on her nerves! Why couldn't Amanda just ignore Tracey like everyone else did?

But this was the least of her problems at the moment. She was still in the state of disbelief she'd woken up to that morning. When she'd realized she was still Tracey Devon a full twenty-four hours later, she'd been engulfed by panic. Was it possible that this was a permanent situation? She couldn't bear to even contemplate the notion. It just couldn't be – this couldn't happen to her. Somehow she'd find a way out of this body.

Madame greeted her with a smile – the first smile that had been aimed in her direction all day. 'Tracey, you're here two days in a row! That's great!'

Again, Amanda was puzzled by the enthusiastic response to her appearance. Was Tracey out so much? She remembered class the day before, when the roll was taken. That teacher had acted surprised to find her there. None of her other teachers made a big deal about it – but then, none of the other teachers took roll. Those teachers probably didn't even notice if Tracey was there or not.

Maybe Tracey was in the habit of just cutting *this* class, the gifted one. But why would she cut the one class where she got treated decently? Or, at least, *noticed*. Anyway, she didn't think Tracey was the type to break rules. And where would she go?

Ken walked into the class, and Amanda gazed at him in a whole new light. He was still cute, he was still cool, but if she'd understood what he'd said in class the day before, Ken heard the voices of dead people. Or at least, he *said* he did. Whether dead people really talked to him or Ken just imagined he heard them, either way it gave Amanda the creeps.

The next to walk in – well, roll in, actually – was Charles. Charles, who seemed to be able to make things move just by looking at them. That could be a useful talent, Amanda thought. Sitting at the dinner table, you wouldn't have to ask anyone to pass the salt. All you'd have to do was look at the shaker. She wondered if he had to use the remote when he watched TV or if he could change the channels with his mind.

On the other hand, his 'gift' was sort of scary. Yesterday, one of those flying books could have hit her right in the face. And what if she'd been sitting under a hanging lamp? Charles could have made it drop right down on her head. She made a mental note to avoid attracting his attention. She didn't really think it would be a problem – Tracey seemed to be very skilled at avoiding attention. Maybe *that* was her gift.

Emily and Sarah were the next to enter the room.

Amanda hadn't quite figured out what kind of special talents they had. All she'd really noticed the day before was that Emily said strange things and Sarah was totally unreadable. Martin was right behind her. All she knew about him was that he could hurt people, but she didn't know *how*.

The little round-faced boy entered. Amanda knew nothing about him, not even his name. And finally came Jenna, who knew what people were thinking.

As she glanced at Jenna, she saw that Jenna was staring directly at her, and there was the oddest expression on her face. *Ohmigod, she's trying to read my mind!* Amanda realized. Frantically, she tried to imagine what Tracey might think about in class. She would probably be depressed, thinking about all the people who had ignored her so far that day – her parents, the bus driver, kids at school. Or maybe she'd be thinking about the person who hadn't ignored her – the girl everyone thought was Amanda Beeson. It dawned on her that she really deserved the title Queen of Mean . . .

Oh no, she was thinking like Amanda! Quickly, she turned her thoughts to Tracey's seven little sisters and tried to remember their names. Sandie, Mandie, Candie . . . Blandie? No, that couldn't be right.

'Good afternoon, class,' Madame said. 'As you recall, yesterday we were discussing Ken's current problem. A man who believes he was murdered by his wife wants Ken to inform the police. Ken does not want to get involved, and he's right to feel that way. Why is he right?'

Martin's hand flew up and he waved it wildly.

'Yes, Martin?'

'He's right because the police wouldn't believe him. No one believes any of us. When I tell people what I can do, they just laugh at me, so then I have to prove it to them. And everyone gets really mad at me.'

Ken spoke. 'Martin, maybe it's better if you don't tell them. Then they won't laugh, and you won't have to prove anything, and no one will get mad at you.'

Madame smiled at Ken. 'Very good advice, Ken. But, Martin, you did answer my question. Ken is doing the right thing by not telling the police, because he wouldn't be believed. You have to remember that ordinary people – people who are not gifted – don't believe in the kind of talents you have. What could happen if any of you tell people what you can do? Emily?'

There was no response.

'*Emily!*'

'Huh? I mean, excuse me, Madame, what did you ask me?'

Madame spoke sternly. 'Emily, you *must* keep your mind here, in class.'

'I'm sorry, Madame. It's just that, well, I keep seeing an earthquake, and I think maybe it's going to happen tomorrow, but I don't know *where*.'

Madame shook her head. 'Emily, you're supposed to try to *control* your visions, not elaborate on them.'

'But if I know where the earthquake's going to happen, I could warn the people there so no one would get hurt.'

Charles offered a comment. 'They wouldn't listen to you. It's like Martin just said – they wouldn't believe you. They'd just think you were nuts.'

Emily persisted. 'But they'd find out later that I was right.'

'And then what would happen to you, Emily?'

Madame addressed the entire class. 'What would happen to any of you if people accepted the fact that you have a gift? Sarah, what do you think could happen to you?'

Sarah's permanent smile actually wavered. 'Someone might ask me to do terrible things for them.'

'You could always say no,' Charles said. 'That's what I'd do.'

Jenna piped up. 'Oh yeah? What if that person was holding a gun to your head while he asked you?'

'Easy,' Charles replied. 'I'd make the gun fly right out of his hand. And Sarah could do better than that. She could make the person put the gun to his own head and blow his own brains out!'

'I would never do that!' Sarah cried out.

'Maybe you *wouldn't*,' Jenna said, 'but you *could*.'

Madame took over. 'The point is, if people found out what you can do, they'd try to use you for their own purposes. You'd be taken away somewhere and studied, tested, examined. Imprisoned, possibly. Tracey, do you have an opinion about this?'

Amanda didn't know what to say. She was still

trying to come to terms with what she'd just learned – that Emily could see into the future. That Sarah could control what people did. And she was bewildered by the way Madame was talking to them – she sounded like a parent reminding children why they shouldn't talk to strangers. It was a strange attitude for a teacher. And she still didn't know what she herself – no, what *Tracey* – could do.

Madame was waiting for an answer, and she was gazing at Tracey with a slight pucker on her forehead.

'Uh, no, I don't have an opinion, Madame.'

'Typical!' Charles snorted.

From his reaction, Amanda gathered that Tracey didn't say much in this class. That was fine with her.

Madame continued. 'Let's get back to Ken's situation. Yesterday I asked you to think about a moment when you successfully controlled your gift. It's possible that Ken could benefit from your experience. Who wants to tell us about a particular incident? Emily? *Emily!*'

'Yes, Madame, I had a good experience last weekend. My aunt and her boyfriend were having dinner with us. They're getting married in a couple of months, and they were talking about where to go on their honeymoon. My aunt wants to go to Bermuda and I don't even know where that is, exactly, but I closed my eyes and concentrated and I saw a tropical storm going on there in two months, just around the same time as their honeymoon!'

Madame appeared concerned, but Amanda didn't think this had anything to do with the aunt's honeymoon. 'Did you tell your aunt?'

'Not exactly. I told them that I knew some people who went to Jamaica for their honeymoon, and they liked it a lot. So then they started talking about Jamaica. And it turns out that my aunt's boyfriend always wanted to go to Jamaica, so they're changing their honeymoon plans!'

'Hey, that's pretty cool,' Ken commented. 'You got them out of the tropical storm, but you didn't have to reveal anything about yourself.'

Madame nodded slowly. 'Yes, that was creative thinking, Emily. But you were still taking a risk. You might have raised suspicions.'

'But she's my aunt, Madame! She wouldn't want to hurt me.'

'Not intentionally, perhaps,' Madame said. 'But the danger is there, Emily, and you must always be aware—'

'Wait a minute,' Jenna broke in. 'How about all those other people in Bermuda? Some of them might be on honeymoon too.'

'But I can't help everyone!' Emily cried out.

'Why not?' Charles challenged her. 'If you had seen the future before I was born, you could have told my parents that the doctor was going to make a stupid mistake when he delivered me, and they could have changed doctors, and I wouldn't be in a wheelchair!'

'I wasn't even a year old when you were born!' Emily wailed.

Madame clapped her hands. 'Class, class! That's enough. We're supposed to be talking about *Ken*'s situation today.'

But just then the classroom door opened and in walked the principal, Mr Jackson, with a young woman Amanda had never seen before.

Madame frowned slightly at the interruption. 'Good afternoon, Mr Jackson,' she said politely, but there was an edge to her voice that Amanda found interesting. Whenever the principal came into classrooms, teachers behaved very respectfully and made a big deal out of welcoming him. Something about Madame's voice and expression told Amanda that she wasn't too crazy about Jackson. Maybe other teachers didn't like Mr Jackson, but they certainly never showed it. And once again she was intrigued by how different Madame was from other teachers.

'What can we do for you, Mr Jackson?' Madame asked, but she sounded like she didn't want to do anything at all for him.

The principal's normally solemn face was unusually cheerful. 'It's what *I* can do for *you*, Madame. *And* for your entire class. I would like to introduce you all to Serena Hancock, your new student teacher.'

Madame was clearly taken aback. 'Student teacher? I didn't request a student teacher, Mr Jackson. We've never had a student teacher in this class.'

The principal's face hardened slightly. 'Well, you do now. And I would think you'd be grateful to have the help. Your students are supposedly gifted, isn't that right?'

Madame looked at him cautiously. 'Yes.'

'Well, Ms Hancock has a gift too. She can perform hypnosis.'

To Amanda's eyes, Madame seemed alarmed now. 'And why would my students need to be hypnotized?'

The principal shrugged. 'Special children, special needs, special solutions. I'll leave Ms Hancock with you now.' And he left the room.

Along with the others, Amanda gazed at Ms Hancock curiously. She was actually pretty impressed with this new addition to their classroom. Like most student teachers, she was young, probably in her twenties. Unlike most student teachers, she looked very cool. She had long, thick blonde hair that hung down her back in perfect waves, and a scarlet mouth. Her dress was amazing – short, figure-hugging and printed in bold colours, turquoise and deep violet. As a loyal reader of *Teen Vogue*, Amanda knew that turquoise and deep violet were very big this season.

'Please take a seat, Ms Hancock,' Madame commanded. 'I'm sure you'll want to just observe today.'

The younger woman smiled, revealing perfectly brilliant white teeth. 'Thank you, Madame. But please, call me Serena.' She turned to the students. 'All of you can call me Serena.'

Amanda could completely understand the startled expression that crossed Madame's face. No teachers, not even student teachers, were ever called by their first name at Meadowbrook.

Everyone watched as Serena took a seat at the back of the room. Then they turned back to Madame.

Amanda thought she looked flustered, like she wasn't sure how to proceed. It was an odd expression for Madame – after only two classes, Amanda could tell that the teacher normally had an air of complete confidence. What was she worried about? Did she think she'd lose control of the class to a student teacher? No one ever paid much attention to student teachers.

Finally Madame spoke again. 'I think this is a good time to do some silent reading. I'm sure you've all got books with you. Please take them out now.' She too went to her desk and opened a book.

This was very odd, Amanda thought. It was like she didn't want to continue discussing their gifts in front of the student teacher. But surely the other teachers must know about the weird stuff these students could do? At least Mr Jackson had to know about them – he was the principal! And surely he must have told this student teacher, Serena, before sending her into this room to work with these weirdos.

So why couldn't they go back to what they were talking about? If they did, maybe Amanda could finally learn what Tracey's gift was. Why was Madame suddenly acting like she wanted them all to be quiet? It seemed to her like Madame was always trying to protect them. But protect them from what – or from whom?

They didn't have to read for long. Moments later the bell rang, and Madame dismissed them without even giving them homework to do for the next day.

Amanda gathered her books and walked out into the hall. She headed down the corridor towards her next class, and she didn't realize that Jenna was following her until she whispered in Amanda's ear. 'You're not Tracey.'

Chapter Eight

FOR ONE BRIEF MOMENT, Jenna thought she might have made a mistake. The reaction to her accusation was typical Tracey. The girl who now gazed back at her looked nervous, fearful, and almost ready to cry.

But any doubts in Jenna's head disappeared as 'Tracey's' expression quickly changed. She stared right back at Jenna with a challenging look.

'You're crazy,' the girl said. 'Of course I'm Tracey. Who else could I be?'

This response only confirmed Jenna's suspicion. Tracey would never be confrontational like that.

'You're Amanda Beeson.'

'I am *not*,' she declared hotly, but Jenna didn't have to be a mind reader to see the panic in Amanda–Tracey's eyes.

'Oh yes, you are. You're Little Miss I'm-Too-Cool-For-Words Amanda Beeson. I remember when you and your prissy friends called me a vampire. Huh, I wish! I would have drained your blood by now.'

'You're disgusting and crazy,' the girl-who-wasn't-Tracey said, and turned away.

Jenna grabbed her arm. 'Do your snotty friends know you're a bodysnatcher? What would they say if they found out you're gifted, like the other freaks in the class?'

'They'd never believe you!'

'Let's try it.' Jenna looked around. 'There's Sophie Greene – isn't she one of your friends?'

'And look who she's meeting at her locker,' her classmate retorted. 'Amanda Beeson.'

Jenna's brow puckered as she watched Sophie and Amanda walk down the hall together. 'I don't know who that is. Your clone, maybe. Or a robot. It's not Tracey, that's obvious. She looks too sure of herself.' She looked at Amanda–Tracey appraisingly. 'So you and Tracey didn't change places.'

'No. *That*'s me and *I*'m me and I don't know how

it works, but . . .' Amanda-Tracey stopped suddenly, and Jenna grinned.

'So it's true. I was just guessing, but you really *are* a bodysnatcher. I've heard of people like you, but I never met one before.'

She recognized the flash of anger on her face. She'd seen it before once, in the canteen, when someone spilled orange juice on Amanda's white jeans.

'If you tell anyone,' Amanda said, 'if you dare, I'll—'

Jenna didn't give her the opportunity to complete her threat. 'Don't worry, Amanda, I'm not going to tell anyone. Not *yet*. There's something I'm curious about though. Why would you want to be Tracey?'

'Are you kidding? Do you think I *want* to be in this creepy girl's body? It – it just happened. I was thinking about her, and then . . . poof!'

'Why were you thinking about her? I can't believe the great and wonderful Amanda Beeson gives a damn about poor little Tracey Devon.' Jenna was having a good time teasing Amanda. She'd never had this kind of encounter with a popular girl, and she had to admit it was fun, even if the popular girl didn't look like herself.

'Can't you just go away and mind your own business?' Amanda fumed.

'No. I want to know where Tracey is.'

It was so weird to see a haughty expression on Tracey's face. Jenna had to keep reminding herself that behind the face was super-snob Amanda Beeson.

'I don't know,' Amanda finally admitted.

'You can't hear her thoughts or anything?'

'No.'

Jenna felt a twinge of concern. 'She's not . . . *dead*, is she? Did you kill her when you took over her body?'

'No!' Amanda exclaimed. She hesitated. 'I mean, I don't *think* so.' She bit her lip. 'Wouldn't I feel it if there was someone dead in me?'

'You don't feel her being alive, do you?'

'No.' Amanda looked up at the hall clock. 'The bell's about to ring. I don't want to be late for class.'

'It doesn't matter,' Jenna said. 'Half the time no one sees Tracey anyway.'

Amanda frowned. 'Yeah, what's the deal with that?

Madame keeps saying it's nice to *see* me.'

'You haven't figured that out yet?'

'Figured what out?'

'Tracey's special talent. Her gift.'

'What *is* her gift?'

The bell rang, and the few remaining students in the hall headed off. 'Meet me after school, at the mall, in front of Barnes & Noble.' She couldn't resist one more insult. 'That's a bookstore, in case you don't know. It's next to Style Session, and I'm sure you know where *that* is.'

Feeling unusually pleased with herself, Jenna swaggered off to her next class. For the rest of the school day, her spirits were high. She didn't like anything about Meadowbrook, but she particularly despised Amanda Beeson and her crowd. She was going to enjoy watching Amanda squirm.

Amanda felt sick. To have a freak like Jenna Kelley acting superior to her was almost as bad as being a freak like Tracey Devon. Things were getting worse and worse.

But by the end of the school day, she'd made the

decision to meet Jenna at the mall. Jenna knew Tracey, and Jenna could read minds, so maybe, just maybe, Jenna would be able to help her get out of Tracey's body. She didn't know how Jenna could help, but she figured there was a chance all these weird kids were connected in some way – that they had some sort of special knowledge.

Only, would Jenna *want* to help her? Obviously Jenna despised Amanda, which was natural. Dweebs, nerds and geeks all pretended to hate popular girls, when they actually envied them and wanted to *be* them.

But it seemed like Jenna might care about Tracey. And maybe she'd help Amanda if she thought she was helping Tracey. In any case, Amanda didn't have anything better to do, and going to the mall was preferable to going back to Tracey's home and being ignored.

So when the last bell rang she hurried out of the school and went directly to the corner where she could safely cross the highway to the mall on the other side. And, despite Jenna's snide remark, she knew exactly where Barnes & Noble was. Stupid

Jenna didn't realize that just because a girl was pretty and cool and popular didn't mean she never read a book. In fact, just moments after she arrived at the bookstore, Sophie, Nina and Other-Amanda strolled into the mall. For a second, Amanda froze – what if they saw her with Jenna? And then she almost laughed at her silly thought.

'Why do you look so happy, Tracey?' Nina asked as the group passed her. 'You've got nothing to smile about.'

Now that was interesting, Amanda thought. Usually Nina ignored Tracey like everyone else did. Maybe she was just trying to impress Other-Amanda with her nastiness. Or maybe she was about to challenge Amanda's status as the Queen of Mean! Amanda made a mental note to keep a close eye on Nina.

She was distracted by the arrival of Jenna, who must have overheard Nina's remark.

'Nice friends you've got,' she commented.

'Oh, shut up,' Amanda replied. 'The only reason I'm meeting you here is because maybe you can help me get back into my body. And get Tracey back into hers,' she added quickly. She didn't want Jenna thinking she expected to do *her* any favours.

'We've got to find her first,' Jenna said. 'Which might not be so easy, when you think about her gift.'

'Which is?' Amanda asked eagerly.

But now Jenna was distracted by a group down at the other end of the mall, in front of the department store. 'Want to meet some of *my* friends?' she asked Amanda.

'Not particularly,' Amanda replied, but Jenna took off and Amanda had no option but to follow her. As they got closer to the group, she began to have serious misgivings. Jenna's friends looked like a very creepy bunch.

An older, skinny guy with dyed green hair and a cigarette dangling from his mouth said, 'Hiya, Janie.'

They couldn't have been great friends if he didn't even know her name, Amanda thought. But Jenna didn't seem dismayed. 'Jenna,' she corrected him. 'Yo, Slug.'

Slug? Who had a name like Slug? Amanda couldn't wait to find out what the others were called. The slutty-looking goth girl in black with blood-red lipstick was called Bubbles, while another girl with a shaved head and tattoos up and down her arms was Skank. Jenna introduced the heavy-set guy with the half-closed eyes as Harry. Amanda thought they all looked older, at least eighteen. And they were all extremely ugly.

'This is my friend Am— I mean, Tracey.'

Not since this bodysnatching experience began had Amanda felt so grateful to look like Tracey. She'd absolutely die if anyone saw her real self with people like this.

'What are you up to?' Jenna asked them.

'Gonna hit Target,' Slug said, nodding towards the department store. 'You ever seen one of these?' From his pocket he pulled out an oddly shaped metal gadget.

'What is it – some kind of weapon?' Jenna asked.

Slug made a snorting sound, which Amanda guessed was his version of a laugh. 'Nah. You know those plastic things they stick on stuff so you can't steal them?' He was looking at Amanda now, so she felt obliged to answer.

'It's a security device. The cashier takes it off

after you pay for something. Otherwise it sets off an alarm when you leave the store.'

'Yeah, right. Well, this handy little number takes that plastic thing off. You can walk right out with half the store in your pocket.'

'You'd have to have pretty deep pockets,' Jenna said, and Amanda couldn't help laughing, but no one else got the joke.

'I only got two of these things,' Slug continued, 'but we'll pass 'em around. Then afterwards we'll split the stash. I'm going in to check out the place first, see where the good stuff is. I'll be right back.' Sticking the gadget back in his pocket, Slug strolled into the store.

Amanda turned to Jenna. 'They're going to steal things?'

'Yeah,' Jenna replied in a voice that was just a little bit too cocky. 'You have a problem with that?'

'Well, it's against the law, for one thing.'

That comment got the rest of Jenna's friends laughing, and Amanda could feel Tracey's face getting red. 'Well, you can leave me out,' she said.

'Chicken?' Jenna taunted.

Amanda couldn't care less if Jenna thought she was a coward. What worried her was the idea that this enterprise could end any kind of collaboration between them.

'There's Slug,' Bubbles said. He was just outside the Target door, and he beckoned them closer. Bubbles, Skank and Harry started toward him, but Jenna hung back for a moment.

'You sure you're not up for this?' she asked Amanda.

Before Amanda could reply, she heard another familiar voice behind her.

'Hi, guys! What are you doing?'

It was Emily, from their gifted class. She was alone and carrying a bag from the bookshop.

'Just messing around,' Jenna said.

Emily smiled vaguely. 'I didn't know you two hung out together.'

Amanda wanted to correct that assumption, but she held her tongue. 'What did you buy?' she asked instead.

Emily reached into her bag and pulled out a book. Jenna read the title. '*I Was Marie Antoinette.*'

'She was the last queen of France,' Emily told them. 'Her head was cut off in the French Revolution.'

Jenna snickered. 'Who wrote the book? Her ghost?'

'No, a woman named Lavinia Pushnik. She claims that she was Marie Antoinette in an earlier life.'

Amanda rolled her eyes. 'You don't believe that stuff, do you?'

Emily shrugged. 'I see the future. Maybe she sees the past.'

Now it was Jenna's turn to do some eye-rolling. 'Emily, anyone can see the past. It's called history. You can read it in books.'

'Mmm.' Emily seemed to have stopped listening. Her eyes were glazed over.

'Are you seeing something in the future now?' Amanda asked.

Emily nodded. 'Someone who's just about to win the lottery.'

'Oh yeah?' Now Jenna looked interested. 'My mother plays the lottery every week.'

'Someone in Canada,' Emily murmured. 'Toronto . . . no, Montreal.'

Jenna's face fell. 'Oh. Well, I have to get into Target before all the good stuff is gone.'

'What do you mean?' Emily asked.

'Jenna and her buddies are about to do some shoplifting,' Amanda told her.

Emily's expression changed. 'Don't do it, Jenna.'

Jenna groaned. 'Oh, great! Another goody-goody who's afraid to break the law.'

Emily shook her head. 'Your friends . . . they're going to get caught.'

'You see that?' Amanda asked. 'For real?'

Emily nodded.

Jenna looked sceptical. 'You're just saying that so I won't steal anything.'

'No,' Emily said. 'It's going to happen.'

'I'd better warn them.' Jenna started towards the store.

'No!' Emily cried out. 'You'll get caught too. It's just about to happen.'

Jenna hesitated, and that was a good thing. Because only seconds later, a uniformed guard emerged with Jenna's pals, all in handcuffs. They disappeared behind a door marked 'Security'.

'Wow,' Amanda said in awe. 'How did you know?'

'That's my gift,' Emily said, but she didn't sound particularly proud of it. 'I see things. Only I never know what to do about them.'

'Well, thanks for telling me about that,' Jenna said 'I would have had a one-way ticket back to reform school.'

'I'm glad I helped you,' Emily said, but now her voice was sad. 'I don't get to help people much, mainly because my visions aren't usually very clear. And then — well, it's like Madame says, who's going to believe me? They'll just think I'm nuts.'

Amanda knew that if she wanted everyone to believe that she was Tracey, she should keep her mouth shut. But she couldn't resist a question. 'Could you always do this? See the future?'

'When I was five, I had my first vision. My father was leaving the house to go to work. And I saw that when he got to the end of the driveway, another car was going to come around the corner really fast and hit him hard. But I didn't tell him.'

'Did it happen?' Amanda asked.

Emily nodded. 'He was killed. Don't you remember? I told this story in class.'

'I, uh, must have been out that day,' Amanda said. Emily's story was awful, really depressing, and Amanda wanted to change the subject. Luckily, she spotted someone in the mall who they might find interesting. 'Isn't that the new student teacher?'

Just as they all turned to look at her, the young woman saw them. She waved and started towards them.

'Oh, great! A teacher,' Jenna groaned.

But the young woman seemed very happy to see them. 'Hi, girls! What a coincidence, running into you here!'

Emily said, 'Hello, Miss . . . uh . . .'

'Serena,' the teacher prompted. 'This is so cool! What are you up to?'

Personally, Amanda thought she was overdoing the 'I'm-your-buddy-not-your-teacher' thing. Jenna also looked doubtful. But Emily seemed intrigued.

'We're just hanging out,' she said.

'I am so excited about this job!' Serena told them. Jenna's eyebrows went up. 'Really? Why?'

'Well, it's not just student teaching, is it? I mean, you guys are really different.'

Jenna still looked wary. 'What do you mean, "different"?'

'It's OK,' Serena assured her. 'I know that you are, you know, *special*. And I really want to know you. As friends, not students.'

'But that's what we are,' Emily said. 'Students.'

Serena tossed her head back and laughed, as if Emily had said something uproariously funny. 'Really, guys, I'm not like your other teachers. Madame, she's very nice and all that, but she's *old*. It's not like you can confide in her. I want you to think of me as someone you can really talk to. You can tell me your secrets, your feelings.'

'Madame doesn't like us to talk about ourselves too much,' Emily said.

Serena nodded. 'Yeah, that's kind of sad, isn't it? It must be sort of lonely for you guys, not being able to talk about what's important to you.'

Emily nodded fervently. 'It is.'

She was awfully eager, Amanda thought. Why would anyone want to tell their secrets to someone they'd just met? The woman was so pushy, it was making Amanda uncomfortable.

Jenna seemed to be having a similar reaction. 'I'm out of here,' she announced, and took off.

'I have to go too, Miss – uh, I mean, Serena,' Amanda said. 'Bye, Emily.'

She hurried after Jenna, and caught up with her. 'Wait! You still haven't told me.'

'Told you what?' Jenna asked.

'About Tracey. About her gift.'

'You still haven't worked it out?'

'No.'

Jenna grinned. 'Tracey can disappear.'

Walking home, Jenna was in pretty good spirits for a change. It hadn't been a bad day – not bad at all. In her mind, she kept seeing the look on the face of Amanda-Tracey when she told her she'd worked out who she was. Of course, it would have been more fun to see that stunned expression on the real face of that conceited Amanda Beeson, but this was the next best thing – knowing she'd freaked out the snottiest girl at Meadowbrook. And that incident at the mall had been pretty cool too.

She didn't like Slug and Skank and the rest of them, even though she'd called them her 'crew' when she talked to Mr Gonzalez and she'd told Amanda they were her friends. Actually, she thought they were a bunch of miserable lowlifes. They didn't do anything real, like go to school or work. They just hung around all day, begging on street corners or picking pockets or shoplifting. They were filthy and not too intelligent, though she had to admit she liked Bubbles's goth look, which was an extreme version of her own.

They didn't really live anywhere, though sometimes they'd squat in an abandoned house or apartment until someone moved in or the police threw them out. Lots of times they slept on the benches in the train station, and that's how Jenna knew them. There were times when she also hung around the train station, when she couldn't bear to go home.

But she probably would have gone into Target with them if Emily hadn't come along and predicted what was going to happen. Like the rest of the kids in class, Emily didn't have a whole lot of control over her gift, so Jenna had truly lucked out.

A light rain began to fall, but that wasn't what suddenly dampened her spirits. She'd turned onto the street where she lived.

The three tall brick apartment buildings took up the whole street. Brookside Towers, they were called, which was a joke – there was no brook alongside the structures, and 'towers' made them sound like castles or something. In reality, Brookside Towers was public housing, packed with all kinds of people who had only one thing in common – not much money.

Jenna suspected the buildings had been ugly when they were built, and they were even uglier now, covered with graffiti and gang symbols. There were a lot of cracked windows, and cardboard had replaced the glass in some of them. The grounds around them weren't exactly gardens: any grass that might be there was covered with junk – rubbish bags, an old refrigerator, a broken bicycle.

There were some good people at Brookside Towers. Jenna thought of Mrs Wong down the hall, who had put up window boxes full of geraniums.

Then some boys had managed to climb up to her window and destroy them. Mrs Wong had cried . . .

No, Brookside Towers wasn't a very nice place to live. Sometimes, when her mother was sober and feeling optimistic, she'd make promises to Jenna.

'No matter how broke I am, I'm going to buy a lottery ticket every week. And one of these days, baby, our ship will come in, and I'll buy us a nice house in a nice neighbourhood. If I keep buying tickets, I've got to win sooner or later, right? I mean, it's like that law of averages or whatever it's called.' Jenna never bothered to tell her mother that she was wrong, that the law of averages meant that it was highly unlikely she'd ever win at all.

Jenna didn't despise her mother. She was just a poor, weak woman whose husband – Jenna's father – had walked out on her when she got pregnant. And she could feel better about herself only by getting drunk or high. She wasn't hateful – just very, very sad.

Jenna thought you could *feel* the sadness when you walked into the apartment, even when her mother wasn't home, like now. She took advantage of her mother's absence to pick up the empty bottles, sweep the floors, and wash the dirty dishes in the sink. Hunting in a cabinet, she found a jar of peanut butter and some stale crackers to spread it on.

The cable bill hadn't been paid, so the TV was worthless. With nothing else to do, she got out her homework. She had a lot of reading to do, but that was OK. Jenna liked to read.

Of course, she couldn't tell anyone that. It was bad for her image . . .

CHAPTER NINE

AT FIRST AMANDA DIDN'T think it sounded so bad, and on the way home she contemplated this bit of news. So Tracey could turn invisible. That explained why she seemed to be absent a lot and why Madame kept saying it was nice to *see* her. And maybe that also explained why Tracey looked blurry in her mirror reflection and fuzzy in photographs.

Now, the question was, what could Amanda do with this knowledge? This gift opened up a whole new range of possibilities.

What if she just disappeared? Took off until all this was over? Maybe she could sneak on to an aeroplane, go to an exotic vacation place and lie on the beach doing nothing. Could invisible people get a tan?

She could stay in the fanciest hotels without

paying. She wondered what happened when an invisible person ate – did the food just disappear? Or could you see it digesting in their invisible stomach? That would be pretty gross.

Or she could hang around some famous people, like actors or rock stars, and see what they were really like. Or even just go to her very own home, and see what her other self was up to . . .

But ultimately, she had to remember the sad truth of the matter. These gifted kids – they couldn't control their gifts. Sometimes Jenna couldn't penetrate minds, and Emily's visions of the future weren't always clear. For Tracey, disappearing probably just happened – she couldn't just snap her fingers and disappear.

So she went back to Tracey's house and spent another yucky Tracey-style evening. At dinner, she pushed the food around her plate while each of the Devon Seven were asked about their day and the parents exclaimed over how adorable they were. No one noticed that Tracey wasn't even eating.

After dinner she went to Tracey's room, where she did some homework and read a book she'd brought home from the school library. And then she remembered Tracey's diary. Maybe Tracey had gone on some interesting adventures while she was invisible. She retrieved the notebook and opened it at random.

'Dear Diary, Everybody thinks the Devon Seven are so cute. I'm not cute.'

That was certainly true, Amanda thought. She turned a few more pages.

'Dear Diary, My little sisters turned three today. They're getting bigger. I feel as if I'm getting smaller.'

Now that sounded interesting, Amanda thought. Was this when she started disappearing? She turned a page.

'Dear Diary, Mom and Dad don't look at me any more. They only see the Seven. I might as well be invisible.'

So it definitely was the septuplets Tracey had written about when she wrote 'Sometimes I hate them'. Amanda couldn't blame her. They took all the attention away from Tracey. But now Tracey was about to become invisible, which should make up for it all.

Eagerly, Amanda turned the next page.

'Dear Diary, Sometimes I think I'd like to get a haircut. And some new clothes. But what's the point? Nobody would notice. Nobody sees me now. I'm nothing.'

Amanda was infuriated. Without even bothering to shut the notebook, she tossed it across the room. So Tracey felt sorry for herself. In all fairness, Amanda knew she was probably entitled to a little self-pity. But Amanda certainly didn't want to have to read about it.

At least Tracey was starting to make sense. From the photos she'd seen, Amanda knew Tracey must have been the centre of her parents' life when she was born, as most babies were. But once the seven girls were born, she grew less and less important in her parents' eyes. She must have felt that. And if you felt like nothing at home, you'd feel like nothing at school too. It wasn't just shyness that made Tracey disappear – Tracey faded away from lack of attention. And all because of those wretched little septuplets.

Later, lying in Tracey's bed, she thought about her own home, her own parents. Being an only child, she always complained that her mother and father made too much of a fuss over her, watched her too closely and wanted to know everything about her. She was a star at home, which was nice, but it could get a little tiresome – there was such a thing as too much attention. Surely there had to be a happy medium between what she had and what Tracey had.

The next day, Friday, started off as a typical Tracey day. The bus doors closed in her face and she had to walk to school. That made her late arriving at her homeroom for roll call, but no one even noticed.

In Tracey's English class they were reading *Romeo and Juliet*, and Amanda had something she wanted to say – about how Romeo should have felt for Juliet's pulse and then he'd know she wasn't really dead and he wouldn't kill himself and she wouldn't kill herself and they could live happily ever after. But no matter how many times she raised her hand the teacher didn't call on her, not even when she flapped her arm wildly in the air.

It was at lunchtime that she realized what was going on. She was looking for a place to sit, an empty table. As she looked around the crowded, noisy canteen, she realized that she had accidentally paused right next to her own special table, where Britney and Sophie and her other self were gathered. They had to have seen her, but nobody insulted her, not even Amanda herself. That was when she knew she had become invisible.

She hurried out of the canteen to go to the bathroom and confirm this in a mirror. How strange it felt, to be looking at yourself and seeing nothing. And how long would it last?

She left the bathroom and ambled down the corridor. It was kind of cool, to stroll right in front of a hall monitor and not be asked to show a pass. She could walk right out of the building and no one would stop her. But where could she go? In a way, it was too bad she wasn't a gangster like Jenna. She could do a lot of shoplifting in this condition.

She decided to stop at the library and pick out some books. But on the way there, passing the principal's office, the door was slightly ajar and she heard Madame talking to Mr Jackson. She sounded upset, and Amanda paused to listen.

'I don't like this arrangement at all, Mr Jackson. We have discussions of a highly personal nature in that class. My students will not be comfortable talking in front of a total stranger.'

'Serena won't be a stranger for long,' the principal countered. 'And they'll learn to be comfortable with her. To be perfectly honest, Madame, I'm not comfortable with the way you conduct that class. I realize your students are, uh, *unusual*, but that doesn't mean they shouldn't have the usual classroom experiences.'

Madame's voice rose a notch. 'But surely you can understand that their special circumstances require an element of privacy!'

'What exactly makes them so special, Madame?'

There was a moment of silence. Amanda wished she could see Madame's expression.

'You know I'm not at liberty to discuss the details of these children,' she said finally.

Mr Jackson made a grunting noise. 'All I know is that two years ago you showed up here with a letter from the superintendent of schools, a mandate authorizing you to start a special class, with very little information as to what kind of special students would be invited to join the class. Obviously your students are not particularly brilliant, nor are they mentally challenged. All I can see is the fact that they have problems.'

'Gifts.'

'Yes, I know that's what you call them. Others might call them delusions. All I know is that someone believes these kids have . . .' he paused, as if he was searching for the right words, '. . . unusual capabilities. Strange powers or something. Mind reading, fortune-telling – am I correct?'

Amanda couldn't hear Madame's response. Maybe she didn't respond at all, because the next sound she heard was the principal's long sigh.

'And I know that you are not required to share all the information with me. But whatever bizarre *gifts* these kids have, I think you're becoming overprotective of them, Madame. Perhaps a little . . . possessive?'

Madame replied to this. 'I have to be possessive. They need to be protected.'

'But protected from whom? From other students?

From teachers? From me? Surely you're not suggesting that they're in danger here at Meadowbrook?'

'Danger can come in many forms, Mr Jackson. My job is to prepare these students to defend themselves.' Her voice rose. 'No, it's more than a job, it's a mission. I'm trying to teach these children how to cope. And you have no authority over me!'

'If you're going to shout, Madame, please shut the door.' Madame obeyed quickly, and Amanda didn't have enough time to slip inside before the door closed. Too bad, because this was getting interesting. Madame certainly took her job seriously. And Amanda still wasn't completely sure what that job was.

She forgot about the library and roamed the halls looking for something else of interest to listen to or observe unnoticed. When she saw Katie and Britney with hall passes, she followed them to the bathroom. At least she could catch up on the latest gossip.

She watched longingly as her two friends went through the ritual they always performed after lunch. They emptied their make-up bags in a sink and then scrutinized their faces in the mirrors to see what elements were in need of repair. And, of course, they gossiped.

But it was a shock to hear what they were talking about today. 'Amanda is really getting on my nerves lately,' Britney said.

Amanda was stunned. Britney turned and looked around the bathroom. 'Is anyone in here?'

Katie moved over to the stalls and looked under the doors. 'No one's here.'

'I just had a feeling someone was listening to us.' Britney resumed the conversation. 'Amanda just thinks she's all that, you know? OK, so she got some new red ballet flats. Did she really have to keep telling us how much they cost?'

'She does that all the time,' Katie said. 'It's like she wants to make sure we know she's got more money than we have. That is so uncool.'

Amanda was aghast, and completely bewildered. What was the point of getting new things if everyone didn't know they were expensive? She'd always thought they were impressed by the cost of her clothes.

'And the way she was making fun of Shannon's shirt, with the flowers on it, just because her mother embroidered the flowers herself,' Britney continued. 'Between us, I thought it was kind of cute.'

'So did I,' Katie said.

So this was how her good friends talked about her when she wasn't around! Just then, her other self came into the bathroom.

'Guys, I forgot to show you,' she said. 'Look what I got at Sephora yesterday.'

Amanda felt like she was watching a home movie as this Amanda opened her bag and pulled out a little case. 'It's a make-up travel kit, with everything you need all in one place. Look, it's even got little brushes and everything. It was super-expensive, but I just had to have it.'

'Oh, I love it!' Britney exclaimed.

'It's so cute!' Katie gushed.

Two-faced creeps, Amanda thought. Another girl came into the bathroom, and she took advantage of the open door to escape. With nothing else to do, she headed to the gifted class.

She was the first student to arrive, but Madame was there with the student teacher.

'I'd like to start the hypnosis sessions today,' Serena was saying.

'I'm sorry,' Madame said, though she didn't sound sorry at all. 'I've got a complicated lesson plan. There won't be time today.'

Serena smiled. 'Mr Jackson said I could take the students individually out of the classroom, and work with each one in the empty room next door. So it won't disrupt the entire class.'

'But the student you take out will miss what the rest of the class does,' Madame objected.

'But think of the potential benefits, Madame. Your objective is to teach your students to deal with their . . . their peculiarities. There's been a lot of research that indicates that hypnosis can have a real impact on a person's ability to control bad habits.'

Amanda took advantage of her invisibility to scoot around the desk and take a good long look at Serena. Personally, she couldn't see why Madame was so nervous around her. OK, Serena was pushy, but why did Madame look so suspicious? Was she afraid that the students would like Serena as a teacher more than they liked her? But Madame didn't seem like the kind of person who cared about popularity.

Other students were arriving, and Madame spoke more softly to Serena. 'Their *habits*, as you call them, are not necessarily bad.'

'Well, you know what I mean,' the student teacher said. 'And I do have Mr Jackson's permission to carry out these sessions.'

Madame's lips tightened. Then she nodded. 'All right, Ms Hancock.'

'Call me Serena.'

Madame turned and surveyed the room. 'Charles, please go with Ms Hancock to the room next door.'

'I don't want to go with her,' Charles muttered.

'Now, Charles, there's nothing to be afraid of,' Serena said brightly. 'This will be fun!' She grabbed the handles of Charles's wheelchair and pushed him out of the room.

'Is she going to hypnotize Charles?' Emily asked when they were out of the room.

'She's going to try,' Madame said. 'Not all people

can be hypnotized. Unique people may have . . . unique reactions.'

Amanda thought she could see a little smile on the teacher's face, but it disappeared too fast for her to be sure.

'Now, let's see,' Madame continued, surveying the room. 'We have some absentees today. Martin has the flu – his mother called the office. And Tracey—'

Jenna interrupted. 'Tracey's here, Madame. I can tell.'

'Thank you, Jenna, but I must remind you that it isn't appropriate to read Tracey's mind without her permission. Or anyone else's, for that matter. Now—'

But once again she was interrupted, this time by a crash that practically made the whole room vibrate. 'Oh dear,' Madame said. 'I think hypnosis has brought out some anger in Charles.'

Sure enough, seconds later their door swung open and a furious Serena stormed in, followed by Charles, who was wheeling himself this time.

'That – that brat made my chair fall over!' the student teacher fumed.

'Oh my, that wasn't very nice, Charles,' Madame

scolded, but her tone was mild, and Amanda could have sworn she saw a glint of satisfaction in her eyes. 'Ms Hancock – I mean, Serena – why don't you take Ken today instead?'

Serena glared at her. 'No, I think I'll have *her*.' She pointed to Emily.

'As you wish,' Madame said coolly.

Serena's expression changed dramatically, and she smiled sweetly at Emily. 'Is that all right with you, Emily?'

Amanda watched them leave, and wondered if Serena's hypnosis might help *her*. Maybe if she was unconscious, Serena could reach the real Tracey inside her and get her to come back out . . .

There was a voice at her ear. 'Or maybe hypnosis would turn you into Tracey for good. Wouldn't you just love that?'

Shut up, Jenna, she thought fiercely. *And don't make fun of me. Help me!* After a second, she concentrated as hard as possible on one additional word. *Please?*

It seemed to take forever before the girl sitting behind her whispered in her ear again.

'OK.'

CHAPTER TEN

'M NOT DOING IT for *you*,' Jenna said.
'I want to help Tracey. I'm sure she's
not thrilled about this either.

She read Amanda's mind. *Yeah, right, whatever.*
Just do it.

'And don't give me orders! I don't care if you're
Miss All That Amanda Beeson – you can't boss me
around.'

She was almost surprised to hear the tiniest
touch of meekness in Amanda's mental response.
OK, sorry. Where are we going?

'My place.'

I hope none of her scummy friends are there.

'Don't worry, nobody's home,' Jenna snapped.
This was the day the new lottery tickets were
issued. Her mother was always willing to stand in

line for hours. She thought putting in the effort would bring her more luck.

Could you please *turn off your little gift? I'm entitled to the privacy of my own thoughts.*

'Like I'd be interested in anything going on in *your* feeble little mind.'

Then stop reading it!

Jenna tried. But there was no missing Amanda's reaction when they turned the corner.

Ohmigod, she lives in Brookside Towers! Yuck!

Jenna gritted her teeth. It was too bad Amanda couldn't read *her* mind – she would hear herself being called every nasty, dirty name ever invented. But she kept telling herself – just as she'd told Amanda – she was doing this for Tracey, and she kept her mouth shut.

But why was she so intent on helping Tracey? It wasn't as if they were great friends; they knew each other only through the gifted class. And she didn't know anything about Tracey, since the girl didn't say much at all, even when she was visible.

Unsure as to whether Amanda was alongside her

or behind her, she held the door to her apartment open. She knew Amanda was inside when she sensed her discomfort at finding herself in such shabby conditions.

'It's not the kind of castle you're used to,' she declared, 'but it's clean.'

What's her problem? I wasn't even thinking anything.

Well, maybe it was just what she expected Amanda to feel. 'Sit down,' Jenna ordered, and pointed to the sofa. She pulled up a chair. 'Are you facing me?'

Is she going to try to hypnotize me?

'No, I'm not into that.' She caught a glimpse of something else in Amanda's head, and couldn't help nodding. 'Yeah, I think Serena's kind of weird, too.' Then she frowned. Was she actually finding something in common with this snob?

'How did you get into Tracey in the first place?' she asked. She caught a glimpse of a response in Amanda's mind, but it was obvious to her that Amanda was trying to put one over on her.

'You *cared* about her? Ha! Amanda Beeson cares only about Amanda Beeson.' She concentrated on getting deeper into Amanda's thoughts, but there wasn't much to learn. Amanda was now mentally counting backwards from one thousand. Obviously, she was trying to keep Jenna from learning more about her.

'OK, OK, I get it,' Jenna said. 'And I don't want to know you either. Like I said, this is for Tracey.' She took a deep breath.

'Tracey, I know you're in there. It's not your fault that this – that Amanda took over your body. But you've got to be strong now. Come out, get rid of her, take over.'

Does she have to make it sound so violent?

'Stop thinking!' Jenna barked. 'I can't reach Tracey if you keep interrupting. Tracey, I'll bet you can hear me. I don't know why you go invisible like you do. Maybe you're just shy or something. But now it's like you've completely disappeared, and that's worse. Now, if you come out, Amanda can go back into her little princess world and you can come back into yours and everything will be normal, OK? Tracey? *Tracey!*'

She concentrated as hard as she could, but all she

could sense was Amanda trying very hard to think of nothing.

'I give up. I can't hear her at all.'

You can't give up, I have to get out of here! Bring her back!

'I just said I can't! Look, did it ever occur to you that maybe she doesn't want to come back?'

You mean I could be stuck inside Tracey forever?

Jenna was spared from answering that when the door to the apartment opened. 'Hi, honey pie!' her mother squealed.

'Hi, Mom.' Jenna glanced nervously in the direction where Amanda had been sitting.

'Guess what? I bought fifty lottery tickets!'

It was clear to Jenna that her mother must have had a few drinks before making the decision to buy more than her usual one.

'Why, Mom?'

'Honey, I just had this *feeling*. This is it! This is our week!'

'Sure, Mom.' She glanced back at the sofa and knew Amanda was still there. *Get out of here*, she thought fiercely, but of course Amanda wasn't a mind reader. All Jenna got in return was Amanda's reaction to her mother.

'I'm starving, Jenna, honey. Is there anything to eat?'

'No, Mom. I was waiting for you to come home with some money so I could go to the store. I'll go now.'

Her mother's face crumpled. 'But I don't have any more money, Jenna. I spent it all on lottery tickets.'

Jenna sighed. 'It's OK, I think I've got five bucks stashed away. I'll get us something.' Then she stiffened as she became aware of something very different coming from Amanda. It wasn't disgust Amanda was feeling, or even distaste. It was pity. Amanda was feeling sorry for her.

Jenna clenched her fists in rage. Even in her foggy state, her mother could see something was wrong.

'Honey, you OK?'

What could Jenna say? That she desperately wanted her mother out of the room so she could tell Amanda what she could do with her pity?

Then yet another realization hit her. How could she be reading pity in Amanda's mind? Girls like

Amanda Beeson never thought about anyone but themselves. It was impossible that Amanda could be feeling sorry for her. So maybe, maybe, she was actually making contact with Tracey!

And then she realized that Amanda was leaving. 'Wait!' she cried out.

Her mother looked at her strangely. 'What did you say, honey?'

Jenna sighed and tried to hold on to Amanda-Tracey's thoughts as she went out the door. The pity was still there, but another feeling had joined it – something that didn't make sense at all to Jenna. It seemed to her like . . . fear.

Now what was *that* all about?

Chapter Eleven

AMANDA DIDN'T PAUSE for a breath until Brookside Towers was way out of sight and she felt reasonably safe. She couldn't believe how close she'd come to even more serious trouble back there. The last thing she needed was to feel sorry for Jenna. Becoming Jenna Kelley was no more appealing to her than being Tracey Devon. Jenna certainly didn't have a better life than Tracey. At least Tracey lived in a nice house where there was food in the kitchen. And at least Tracey had a couple of normal parents.

Well, sort of normal. They were normal to the septuplets. But for Tracey . . . Amanda couldn't quite figure it out. OK, Tracey was a nerd and she didn't have any friends, but weren't parents supposed to love their kids unconditionally, even if they were pathetic? The more she thought about it, the more she realized that it wasn't the fault of the Devon Seven that Tracey was such a mess. It was her parents' fault.

At that moment she wasn't in any mood to face those parents, even if they couldn't see her. And she decided to take advantage of her invisibility by paying a visit to a place she'd been trying not to think about.

Had it really been less than a week since she'd been in her own home? It felt like forever. It was funny how she'd forgotten what a pretty house it was. She stood there, at the end of the drive, and just admired it.

Then she caught her breath. There she was – Amanda Beeson, accompanied by Katie and Britney, walking right by her. *Boy, if she only knew what they'd been saying about her in the bathroom,* Amanda thought. She picked up her pace so she could enter the house with them.

Her very own mother came into the hall to greet them. 'Hello, darling. Hi, girls.'

Other-Amanda didn't bother with greetings.

'Mom, we're starving. Is there anything to eat?'

'Of course there is! I made chocolate-chip cookies for you.'

'Yum,' Katie and Britney chorused, but Other-Amanda stamped her foot. 'Mom! You know I'm on a diet! Why did you have to go and make cookies?'

'Amanda, darling, there's no need for you to be on a diet,' her mother protested as she followed them into the kitchen.

'Oh, what would *you* know?' Other-Amanda muttered.

Jeez, was she rude or what? Amanda thought. But wasn't that what she would normally say?

'Girls, would you like some milk with those cookies?' Amanda's mother asked, opening the refrigerator and taking out a carton.

'*Mom!* Could we have some privacy, puh-leeze!'

Amanda could see the irritation on her mother's face, but the woman didn't say anything. She probably didn't want to embarrass her daughter by scolding her in front of her friends. That was the kind of thoughtful person she was.

As soon as her mother left, Other-Amanda said,

'Guys, did I tell you what I did to Tracey Devon in PE? I told her I saw an insect crawling out of her hair!'

Britney and Katie burst out laughing. After what she'd heard her friends say in the bathroom that day, Amanda knew they were faking their enthusiasm for Amanda's meanness. They were such hypocrites! And she didn't want to listen to it any more. She started for the door, and then had another thought. She ran up the stairs to her very own room, went into the closet, and grabbed her favourite red ballet flats. It wasn't really stealing, she told herself. After all, they were hers.

By the time she got back to Tracey's house it was after six, and since she was still invisible nobody could see that she was home. But her absence clearly wasn't having any effect on the household. In fact, there was an event going on – a reporter and a film crew were there. The Devon Seven were all dressed in identical pink dresses. Tracey's mother had obviously been to the beauty salon, and even Tracey's father had come home early from work.

They were all gathered in the living room, and

Amanda hovered in the corner to see what was going on. An attractive woman was standing in front of a camera and speaking.

'The impact of multiple births on a family is enormous, financially and emotionally. Mrs Devon, what did the arrival of septuplets do to your life?'

Tracey's mother uttered a tinkling little laugh. 'Well, as you can imagine, our lifestyle certainly changed. George and I used to go out to dinner frequently, and to the theatre. We can't do that as often now.'

'We're going out tonight,' Mr Devon added, 'for the first time since the girls were born.'

'Do you go out less now because of the expense?' the reporter asked.

Mrs Devon looked insulted. 'No, we're quite fortunate in that sense. But it's very difficult to find a babysitter when there are seven children in the house.'

Eight children, Amanda thought. *There are eight children in the house.* Maybe Tracey wasn't an adorable little kid and maybe she didn't require a babysitter, but she had to count for something.

Mr Devon interjected a comment. 'Of course, we don't mind giving up our social life. With seven daughters, it's a party in this house all the time!'

Eight daughters! What was the matter with these people? Didn't they care about Tracey at all? Had they forgotten her? She was really beginning to get irritated with them.

'Do you ever think about having another child?'

'Heavens no,' Mrs Devon said. 'Seven is plenty!'

Now Amanda was fuming and she couldn't keep quiet. 'Eight! You have eight kids!'

There was a shriek from a cameraman, and another man yelled, 'Cut! What happened?'

The cameraman's eyes were huge and he was pointing in Amanda's direction. 'That – that girl! She just popped up out of nowhere!'

So she was visible again. That was a relief. Not to the cameraman though. His face was white and his hand was shaking as he pointed. 'I'm telling you. Look at the tape – she wasn't there a second ago.'

'Don't be ridiculous,' the other man said. 'You just didn't see her come in.' He peered at Amanda. 'Who are you, anyway?'

'I'm Tracey Devon. I'm the Devon Seven's older sister.'

The director seemed taken aback. 'Really?' To the reporter, he said, 'I didn't know there was an older sibling. Did you?'

The reporter turned to the Devon parents. 'I don't think you've ever mentioned another child.' Then, turning back to Amanda, 'What did you say your name is, dear?'

'Tracey.' Amanda glared at Tracey's parents. 'Remember me?'

Mr Devon seemed somewhat befuddled. 'Of course. Don't be silly . . . '

Mrs Devon broke in. 'We thought you'd only be interested in the septuplets. Tracey is our firstborn, she's twelve.'

'*Thirteen!*' Amanda corrected her. That was when it hit her – why Tracey's special gift was disappearing. No one ever saw her, so she just faded away. If no one paid any attention to her, why bother being visible?

'Would you like to be interviewed, Tracey?' the reporter asked. 'I'd like to know how having seven identical siblings has affected your life.'

I don't have a life, Amanda thought. *I mean, Tracey doesn't have a life.* And there wasn't anything she wanted to say about the Devon Seven – she didn't even know them.

'No, I don't want to be interviewed,' Amanda said. If she'd been at her own home, her mother or father would have corrected her: 'No, *thank you.*' She glanced at the parents. As usual, they weren't paying attention. They both just seemed completely puzzled.

The Devon Seven were staring at her too. They were probably amazed to hear her speaking, or to hear other people speaking to *her*. Amanda resisted the urge to stick her tongue out at the little darlings and give them a dirty look. No, it was the parents who deserved the dirty look. Somebody had to take the blame for Tracey's miserable life! Without another word, she left the room and ran upstairs.

Throwing herself on Tracey's bed, she contemplated her situation – *Tracey's* situation. It wasn't right and it wasn't fair. Amanda pounded the pillow in frustration. She even began to wonder if maybe Tracey did have a worse life than Jenna. At least Jenna's mother seemed to love her.

But what really bugged her was the fact that Tracey didn't do anything about it. She just let them ignore her, and went along with it by disappearing.

Then she sat up. Maybe it was Tracey's own fault that her life was crummy. Well, if Amanda was going to have to live as Tracey for a while longer, there was no way she'd follow in Tracey's footsteps.

A little voice inside her asked, *And what if you have to live as Tracey forever?* She forcibly pushed that horrible notion out of her mind. For as long as she did have to be this sad girl, she wasn't going to suffer like Tracey did. It was time for Tracey to take some responsibility for herself.

Amanda remained on the bed, thinking about how to go about doing that. After a while she heard the film people leave and she came out of her room. She still wasn't sure what her first move would be, but she had to do something.

The seven little girls were now bouncing around and making a lot of noise. Mr Devon was trying to hush them as Mrs Devon went to answer the ringing telephone in the kitchen. From the bottom of the stairs, Amanda watched as Mr Devon made futile efforts to get them under control.

'Kandie, stop jumping – you're giving me a headache.'

'I'm not Kandie, I'm Mandie!' the child declared.

Mrs Devon emerged from the kitchen with a stricken look on her face. 'That was Lizzie. She can't babysit.'

'What?' Mr Devon yelled. 'But we're meeting my boss and his wife. We can't cancel now!'

'Well, what do you want me to do?' Mrs Devon shrieked back.

Amanda saw her opportunity. 'I'll babysit.'

Mrs Devon continued with her tirade. 'I can't find a babysitter at the last minute!'

'Yes, you can!' Amanda said more loudly. 'Didn't you hear me? I said I'll babysit.'

She must have spoken even louder than she thought, because she actually got both the parents' attention. But neither of them seemed to have understood.

'What did you say?' Tracey's father asked.

Amanda was getting impatient. 'I *said*, I'll babysit for the girls.'

Tracey's mother stared at her. '*You?*'

'Yes, me. I'm thirteen years old, remember? I can watch them. I'm not saying I'll *entertain* them, but I can make sure they don't play with matches or sharp knives. I can keep them alive till you get back.'

Mr Devon looked at Mrs Devon. 'Why not? We're not going that far. I'll leave my mobile phone number; she can call if there are any problems.'

Mrs Devon still looked uncertain. 'Well . . . I suppose that would be all right.'

'Absolutely,' Mr Devon assured her. 'Thank you for offering, Tracey.'

'Oh, I'm not doing this as a favour,' Amanda corrected him. 'I expect to be paid. How much do you pay Lizzie for babysitting?'

Mr Devon was startled. 'I don't know.' He turned to his wife. 'What do we pay the babysitter?'

'Five dollars an hour,' Mrs Devon said faintly.

'That will be just fine,' Amanda said. 'Five dollars an hour. If I'm not up when you get home, please leave the money on the kitchen table.'

Still looking a little dazed, Mrs Devon nodded.

'Good,' Amanda said. 'I'll be in my room. Let me know when you're ready to leave and I'll get to work.' She couldn't see them as she turned to go back up the stairs, but she could conjure up the pleasant vision of two stunned parents, and it made her smile.

Chapter Twelve

WHEN AMANDA-TRACEY WALKED into class on Monday, Jenna blinked twice. One of those two girls had been very busy that weekend. Not only was Amanda-Tracey visible, she'd been through some kind of transformation.

The outer person was still Tracey but Amanda's influence was showing. The blonde hair was no longer flat and stringy – it had been cut short, to her chin, and it was shining. She was wearing make-up – not a lot, but something made her eyes look bigger, and there was a slick of pink on her lips. And her clothes – they weren't Jenna's kind of clothes, but she knew the other kids at school would consider them cool. This new Tracey wore a long red tunic over cropped jeans, with a short black sweater and red ballerina shoes. She carried her books in a black canvas tote bag over her shoulder.

She was different in other ways too. She held her head up and took long, confident strides into the room. Even Madame looked intrigued.

But before anyone could comment, student teacher Serena came into the room. 'I'd like to see Jenna today,' she announced.

She was addressing Madame, but Jenna responded. 'Maybe I don't want to see *you*.'

'Jenna, that's rude,' Madame murmured.

Emily leaned over towards her. 'It doesn't hurt or anything, Jenna. In fact, it's kind of fun.'

'That's right!' Serena said brightly. She turned to Madame. 'And don't forget, I do have Principal Jackson's authorization to meet with each student independently.'

'I haven't forgotten,' Madame said quietly. 'Jenna, would you please go with Ms Hancock?' And at that moment, for the first time ever, Jenna thought she read a little something in Madame's mind.

And find out what this woman is really up to.

Had Jenna imagined that? Or had Madame

actually allowed Jenna into her head? Jenna decided that maybe a session with the student teacher would be more interesting than the usual boring fifty minutes in class.

'OK.' She followed Serena into the room next door. It was just another classroom, nothing special. Serena directed Jenna to sit down. She did, and then Jenna began to concentrate.

But before she could even begin to penetrate the student teacher's mind, Serena suddenly produced a circular object the size of a dinner plate. 'I want you to look at the red dot in the centre, Jenna.' She pressed something on the plate, and it began to rotate.

Jenna tried to look away, but for some strange reason she couldn't. She couldn't close her eyes either. And any possibility of reading Serena's mind evaporated as her own mind went blank.

No, not *blank* exactly. She was conscious, she was aware of sitting in the room and looking at Serena's plate thing, but there was something happening in her mind. It was being drained . . .

Time passed, but she had no idea how much time.

She couldn't take her eyes off the dot. She could hear just fine though.

'I know all about your special gift, Jenna. But you will not be able to read my mind. If you try to read my mind, you will suffer a severe headache. The pain will become unbearable. This is a post-hypnotic suggestion, Jenna. You will never be able to read my mind. Do you understand?'

Jenna didn't think she could speak or even nod her head. She was completely paralysed. But somehow she must have communicated something, because Serena said, 'Good. Now, please follow me.'

Then she wasn't paralysed at all. She rose and followed Serena out of the room. That was when she realized what had been drained from her mind – her will. She would do whatever this woman said. And she didn't even have enough freedom of thought to feel afraid.

They went down some stairs, walked to the end of a corridor and turned right. Dimly, Jenna knew they were walking into the school canteen.

The last lunch session was still in progress, and she was aware of the noise and the people and the general chaos, but it was as if she wasn't a part of it – more like she was watching the scene on TV. Serena led her across the room to an alcove, where the teachers ate their lunch. The pair of them stood just behind a column, so Jenna could see the teachers but they couldn't see her.

Now Serena was whispering in her ear. 'There is a man at the table. He has light brown hair, and he's wearing glasses. Do you see him?'

Jenna saw him, and even in her strange state she recognized him – Mr Jones, the history teacher.

'During the next few minutes I want you to read his mind,' Serena said. She left Jenna standing there and went over to the table.

With all the noise in the canteen, Jenna couldn't hear anything Serena said to the other teachers. But the student teacher's lips were moving and she was smiling as she sat down next to Mr Jones. And Jenna had no problem at all tuning into the man; in fact, it was the easiest mind reading she'd ever done.

Wow, she's hot! Is she coming on to me? I hope so. I wonder if she's got a boyfriend. If I can get her alone later, I'm going to ask her out.

Serena returned to Jenna. 'We can leave now,' she said, and Jenna followed her back to the room they had been in before.

'Now,' Serena said as they returned to their seats, 'I want you to tell me what Mr Jones was thinking while I spoke to him.'

Jenna had no choice. Like a parrot, she repeated the thoughts she'd read. '"Wow, she's hot! Is she coming on to me? I hope so. I wonder if she's got a boyfriend. If I can get her alone later, I'm going to ask her out."'

Serena smiled. 'Excellent! Now, Jenna, I'm going to take you out of your hypnotic state. Watch the red dot again.'

She held up the object, and this time it spun in the opposite direction. Again, there was the odd passage of time – seconds, minutes, she couldn't tell.

Suddenly, Jenna felt like someone had just tossed a glassful of water in her face. She wasn't wet, but she was very awake.

'That wasn't so bad, was it?' Serena asked cheerfully.

'Was I really hypnotized?' Jenna asked her.

'Absolutely,' Serena assured her. 'Why do you ask?'

'Because I remember everything we did.'

Serena continued to smile. 'Of course you do. This isn't some sort of witchcraft, Jenna, it's psychological science. I'm not attempting to change you – I simply want to understand you – all of you. You kids with your special gifts, you need special attention.'

'But why did I have to—'

She was interrupted by the ringing of the bell. 'That will be all, Jenna. You can go on to your next class.'

Jenna stared at her. But now Serena had opened a notebook and was totally preoccupied with writing something. Clearly, she wasn't going to be answering any questions Jenna might ask, so Jenna left.

But for the rest of the school day, she thought about the odd experience. She'd been with Serena for an entire class period, fifty minutes. But the events that took place could have taken up only ten minutes or so. Had Serena made her do things she *couldn't* remember? Or was the rest of the time occupied with staring at the spinning plate with its stupid red dot?

She kept hoping to run into Emily sometime during the day so she could compare their individual experiences with the student teacher. When school was done for the day, she hurried to the main exit, and positioned herself there to wait for Emily to come out.

When she saw Amanda-Tracey emerge she looked away, expecting that the other girl would do the same. But instead she stopped and spoke.

'What did that student teacher do? Did you get hypnotized?'

'Yeah.'

'What was it like?'

Jenna shrugged. 'No big deal. She didn't make me quack like a duck or anything like that.' She paused. She really wanted to tell *someone* what had happened. 'Actually, it was kind of silly. All she wanted me to do was read another teacher's mind to find out if he wanted to date her.'

'You're kidding! That's all?'

Jenna nodded. 'I'll bet when she hypnotized Emily she asked her if they have a future together.'

Amanda-Tracey laughed. 'And she probably told Charles to push him in her direction.'

Jenna started to laugh too, and then she remembered who she was talking to. She cocked her head to one side and pretended to be noticing something for the first time that day.

'You look different.'

Amanda nodded. 'Yeah, I got a haircut. And I bought some clothes and make-up.'

Jenna sniffed. 'Perfume too. Must be nice having all that money to spend on stuff like that.'

'You think Tracey's parents ever give her money?' Amanda countered. 'They barely know she's alive.'

Now Jenna was interested. 'So what did you do – take the money while you were invisible?'

'*No*. I earned it. Babysitting for the clones. And these aren't exactly designer clothes. I got them at Target.'

'Oh.'

Amanda-Tracey shifted her book bag to her other arm. 'I have to go.'

'Wait, I have to ask you something. No, I mean, I have to *tell* you something.'

'What?' Amanda-Tracey asked.

'Don't ever feel sorry for me.'

'I don't,' Amanda-Tracey replied.

'You did on Friday, at my place. I read it.'

'Well, you read wrong. I never feel sorry for anyone.' With that, Amanda-Tracey sauntered off.

Jenna stared after her. Did Amanda-Tracey mean that? She tried to read her thoughts now, but the gift didn't kick in. So maybe it *was* Tracey she'd made a connection with.

But that didn't feel right either. If Jenna was in Tracey's situation, the only person she'd feel sorry for was herself.

Chapter Thirteen

ARRIVING AT TRACEY'S HOME, Amanda felt like she could be in the Meadowbrook canteen. Chaos reigned.

In the living room, one of the seven girls was lying on the rug, kicking and yelling. Another one was screaming. In the kitchen, one girl spilled her milk and started crying, while another snatched a cookie from her sibling's plate and they started fighting. The mother's help was nowhere in sight, and Tracey's mother looked to be on the verge of hysteria.

'Stop it! All of you, stop it! Go upstairs – it's time for your nap.' None of the septuplets paid any attention to her, just as Tracey's mother didn't pay any attention to the fact that 'Tracey' had just walked in.

Amanda moved into Mrs Devon's line of vision

and spoke loudly. 'What's going on?'

'Lizzie left us!' the woman wailed. 'I've called every agency in town and there's no one available! What am I going to do?'

Amanda surveyed the pandemonium. Having spent a lot of time with the septuplets over the weekend, she had a sense of each personality. She focused on the one who was the bossiest of the group, and at the top of her lungs, she screamed, 'Mandie!'

The septuplet who was taking cookies by force from the others actually looked in her direction.

'Help me,' Amanda ordered her. 'We have to get everyone upstairs. It's storytime.'

Mandie turned to the sweet one, Randie. 'C'mon, we're going upstairs.'

Randie was in the process of twisting Brandie's hair into sloppy plaits, so those two started out together. One by one, the others followed, until there was only one crying child left in the kitchen. Amanda grabbed Tandie's hand and half-walked, half-dragged her out of the kitchen and up the stairs. Mrs Devon brought up the end of the line.

Once they were all gathered in the girls' huge bedroom, Amanda asked, 'Whose turn is it to pick the story?'

'Me! Me!' Vandie cried out. She was the whiney one. Amanda shook her head.

'Let me think . . . Friday night was Brandie, Saturday afternoon it was Kandie's turn, Mandie chose the story on Saturday night . . .'

'I picked the story yesterday,' Randie declared.

'It's my turn! It's my turn!' Vandie shrieked.

'No, I told you yesterday, we're going in alphabetical order. Sandie picks the story today. You come last.'

'That's not fair!' Vandie whined.

'Tough,' Amanda said. 'Life isn't fair. Sandie, go and choose a story.'

As Sandie raced over to the bookcase, Amanda realized that Mrs Devon was looking at her oddly.

'Did you cut your hair?'

'Yes,' Amanda said shortly. 'I had my hair cut on Saturday, with the money you paid me for Friday night.'

'Saturday? I didn't notice it.'

'No,' Amanda said 'you never do. Maybe you should take a look at me once in a while.'

'Here's my story, Tracey,' Sandie announced. The girls gathered in a semicircle as Amanda had taught them to sit over the weekend, and Amanda took her place in the centre, facing them.

As she started reading, from the corner of her eye Amanda could see Mrs Devon standing there, still looking a little dazed, like she'd stumbled into a strange new world. As Amanda read, the septuplets were quiet, and by the time she'd finished the story, they were yawning. With the help of Tracey's mother, she got them into bed for their naps.

Leaving the room together, Mrs Devon continued to look at her like she'd never seen her before in her life. When the doorbell rang, she seemed relieved to have something else to do and hurried to open the door. Amanda was surprised to see Jenna there.

'Um, is Aman— I mean, Tracey home?'

'I'm here,' Amanda said. She joined Mrs Devon at the door. 'Come on in.'

Tracey's mother seemed even more surprised than Amanda. 'Tracey, who is this?'

'A friend of mine, Jenna Kelley,' Amanda replied. 'Come on upstairs to my room, Jenna.'

As they headed to the stairs, she caught another glimpse of Mrs Devon's bewildered expression. Amanda wasn't surprised – Tracey probably hadn't had a visitor since her seventh birthday.

'What are you doing here?' Amanda asked as soon as they were inside Tracey's bedroom with the door closed. That was when she noticed the other girl was carrying a bag.

Jenna wouldn't meet her eyes. She looked past Amanda as she spoke. 'I, uh, I need a place to stay. For a couple of nights. Can I stay here?'

There were twin beds in Tracey's room. 'Yeah, I suppose so. Why do you need a place to stay?'

Jenna shifted her gaze to the other side of the room. 'It's my mother . . . She's got a bunch of friends there. It looks like she's about to have another one of her parties. Which means I won't get any sleep tonight.'

'Oh.' Amanda looked at her curiously. 'Has this ever happened before?'

Jenna nodded. 'Just last week, and the noise kept

me up all night. Sometimes I just go over to the train station and hang out with Slug and those guys. But this time – I don't know, I just don't feel like it.'

'They're probably in jail anyway for trying to shoplift from Target,' Amanda said matter-of-factly. 'You know what, Jenna? I don't think you even like those people. And I'll bet you've never stolen anything in your life.'

Jenna faced her indignantly. 'What makes you think that?'

'Because I don't think you're as bad as you pretend you are. And if you were stealing, you'd probably have more food in your house.'

Jenna's face went white. 'Don't you feel sorry for me. Don't you *dare* feel sorry for me.'

'Don't worry, I don't and I won't,' Amanda said with feeling. 'I don't want your life any more than I want Tracey's.'

Jenna was taken aback. 'Don't tell me you're thinking about snatching *my* body!'

Amanda got up and began pacing the room. 'I don't make those decisions.' Her need to confide, to talk to someone, was irresistible. And at least she didn't care what Jenna thought about her. 'It just happens when I feel really sorry for someone. That's how I got into Tracey's body.'

'Yeah, I read that in your mind, and I still can't believe it,' Jenna said. '*You* feel sorry for people?' Her brow furrowed. 'You're still really Amanda Beeson, the meanest girl at school, right?'

'That's *why* I'm the meanest girl!' Amanda cried out. 'I can't let myself feel sorry for people because I could end up being them! Do you think I *want* to be Tracey Devon? Or you?'

Jenna's mouth was still open. But the only word that came out was, 'Wow!'

'Exactly,' Amanda said. 'See? I'm not the perfect princess you think I am.'

'I *never* thought you were perfect,' Jenna muttered.

'And you're not the gangster I thought you were,' Amanda added.

'I really was in reform school,' Jenna argued.

'Why were you sent there?'

Jenna looked away again. 'I was hanging out with some creeps, and they were dealing drugs. The cops raided the house where we were staying, and someone planted stuff in my pocket.'

Amanda nodded smugly. 'I knew I was right about you. You're a big fake.'

'So are you,' Jenna pointed out.

Amanda shrugged, and there was a long silence. Finally Jenna spoke. 'Remember when I was telling you about Serena and the hypnotism? How she wanted me to find out if this guy was into her? Well . . . I don't think she was really interested in him. There's something else going on. I couldn't read her mind, but I got the feeling she has got secrets.'

Amanda nodded. 'Yeah, I think she's kind of weird too.'

Jenna gazed at her quizzically. 'You know what? We kind of think alike.'

'Yeah, maybe,' Amanda said. 'But that doesn't mean we're going to be friends,' she added hastily.

'Absolutely not,' Jenna assured her.

'Good.' Amanda stood up. 'Let's go to the kitchen and find something to eat. And I'll tell Tracey's mother you're staying for a while.'

'What if she says no?' Jenna asked.

Amanda grinned. 'She's going to have to get used to a different kind of daughter. The kind that always gets her own way.'

CHAPTER FOURTEEN

THERE WERE NO ABSENTEES in the gifted class the next day, so Serena had a full group to choose from.

'Well,' Madame said to her, 'you've seen Charles, Emily, Ken and Jenna, so there's Tracey, Martin, Sarah and Carter to choose from.'

Not me, Amanda thought. Somehow she'd have to avoid being with Serena. Who knew what she might reveal under hypnosis?

Madame wasn't giving Serena the choice. 'I'd like you to spend some time with Carter, Ms Hancock.'

The student teacher had given up asking her to call her Serena. 'Why him?'

Amanda was interested too. Carter was the one student she didn't know anything about. He never spoke, and she had no idea what his special gift might be.

'We think that Carter has amnesia,' Madame explained. 'He was discovered a month ago, wandering the streets, by one of our teachers. We've tested him and he seems very intelligent, but he doesn't speak or communicate in any way. We don't know anything about him.'

'Why is he in the gifted class?' Serena wanted to know.

'We thought Carter might profit from being around other special young people,' Madame said.

Serena didn't look terribly intrigued, but she had a question. 'If he doesn't communicate, how do you know his name?'

'We don't,' Madame said. 'We named him after the place where he was found – Carter Street, on the west side. I think he might really benefit from hypnosis.'

'Oh,' Serena said, but she seemed to have lost interest and continued to gaze around the room. 'Actually, I'd like to see Emily.'

Madame's eyes narrowed. 'But you've already worked with Emily,' she protested.

'There's more work to be done,' Serena insisted.

'But—'

'I do have Principal Jackson's permission,' Serena reminded her.

'All right,' Madame said, but there was no enthusiasm in her tone. 'Emily?'

Emily obediently left the room with Serena. Madame's eyes followed them, and distrust was written all over her face. Amanda turned to look at Jenna. She didn't have to be a mind reader to know that Jenna was wondering about this too.

Finally Madame turned and addressed the rest of the class.

'In the past we've talked about the body-and-mind connection. Today we're going to draw on some yoga exercises, which can be helpful in learning to control your body.'

Amanda was pleased. She hoped that by concentrating on her body, she wouldn't have to think about what was going on inside her head. She joined the class in pushing the desks and chairs away to clear space on the floor for the yoga exercises. Madame produced some mats and spread them around.

But yoga wasn't like doing the kind of exercises they did in PE. Holding positions gave her plenty of unwanted time to think.

My mother is really nice, she thought. *And I'm not very nice to her. What's the matter with me? If I ever get back into myself, I promise I'll be better.*

That was all very well, but she'd have to be herself again before she could make good on her promise. And she had no idea when that would happen – if ever.

Where are you, Tracey? she thought. *Why won't you come back and reclaim your body? I'm making things better for you. You look a lot better. I've made your parents listen to you. If you keep doing what I'm doing, you won't be a great big nothing any more.*

She didn't really expect any response, so she wasn't surprised when she didn't get one. What was the matter with the stupid girl? No, maybe stupid wasn't the right word. Sad – that was Tracey.

Tracey, stop feeling sad. Get . . . get angry!

Still no response. She gave up and concentrated on her body. And she had to admit, when class was over she felt more relaxed than she'd felt in ages.

Maybe it showed, because Madame kept looking at her oddly. And when the bell rang, she called out, 'Tracey, could I see you for a minute?'

Amanda went to the teacher's desk, but Madame said nothing until all the other students had left the room.

Then she gazed at Amanda with an intensity that made her uncomfortable.

'Tracey . . .'

'Yes, Madame?'

The woman shook her head. 'No, you're not Tracey.'

Amanda swallowed, hard. 'I'm not?'

Madame smiled. 'You know you're not.'

Amanda bit her lip. Should she put up an argument? Something about the confidence in Madame's expression told her there was no point. 'Why – why do you think I'm not Tracey?'

'The way you walk, the way you talk, the way you look . . . I've had my suspicions all week. Can you tell me if Tracey is all right?'

'I don't know,' Amanda said honestly.

'Can you tell me who you really are?'

Amanda gulped. 'Do I have to?'

'I can't force you,' Madame said.

'Can I go now?'

Madame nodded. But as she started out of the room the teacher touched her shoulder and she looked back.

'Whoever you are . . . be good to Tracey, OK? There's more to Tracey than meets the eye.'

Amanda had a feeling she wasn't just talking about Tracey's ability to vanish.

'I'm trying,' Amanda said.

When the school day was over, Jenna was waiting for her at the exit. 'What did Madame want?'

'She knows I'm not Tracey,' Amanda said glumly.

'Well, you can't blame her. You're not exactly acting like Tracey. Does she know who you really are?'

Amanda glared at her. 'No, and you better not tell her.'

'My lips are sealed,' Jenna said. 'Can you do me a favour?'

'What?'

Jenna looked uncomfortable. 'This is kind of embarrassing, but . . . when I threw my stuff in my bag yesterday, I forgot something. Something kind of important.'

'So you want to go home and get it?'

Jenna made a face. 'The thing is . . . I don't want to go into the apartment if my mother and her friends are still hanging out. Sometimes these parties go on for days. If my mother sees me, she might start crying and I'll feel awful.'

'You want me to get it for you?'

'Would you?' Jenna asked eagerly.

Amanda shrugged. She didn't have anywhere else she had to be.

When they arrived at the door of Jenna's apartment, they could hear music and voices inside. Amanda hesitated. 'What am I going to tell your mother?'

'Just say you're picking something up for me.'

'But she doesn't know who I am. And she'll want to know why you can't get it yourself. What am I supposed to say?'

Jenna was silent. After a moment, she said, 'Maybe you could be invisible.'

Amanda rolled her eyes. 'Jenna, you know Tracey can't control that.'

'But you're not Tracey,' Jenna countered.

'So what?'

'You're so much stronger than she is. I'll bet if you really wanted to be invisible, you could make it happen.'

Amanda didn't buy it. 'Disappearing is Tracey's gift, not mine.'

'But you're controlling Tracey's body,' Jenna said. 'Maybe you can control her gift.'

Amanda still had doubts. 'What is it I'm supposed to pick up for you anyway?'

Jenna gave her an abashed grin. 'This is the embarrassing part. It's a teddy bear.'

Amanda stared at her in disbelief. Then she burst out laughing. 'See? I knew you weren't so tough!'

Then Jenna was laughing too. 'Yeah, OK, I know it's goofy, but I've always slept with him. Don't tell anyone, OK? It would be very bad for my reputation.'

'No kidding,' Amanda chortled. 'The juvenile delinquent sleeps with her knife, her gun and her teddy bear.'

They were both giggling so hard now they couldn't stop. And they must have been pretty loud, because suddenly a voice could be heard from inside the apartment. 'Is someone out there?'

Then they heard footsteps approaching the door.

Jenna froze. 'It's my mother.'

'Hide,' Amanda hissed.

Jenna ran into the stairwell. Amanda closed her eyes and concentrated as hard as she could. *Help me, Tracey – help me. Help me disappear.* She tried to imagine herself fading away.

She heard the door open and she knew someone was standing there, facing her. Reluctantly, slowly, she opened her eyes.

Jenna's mother looked puzzled. She looked both ways down the hallway and then shrugged.

I did it! Amanda thought gleefully. She edged past Jenna's mother into the apartment, trying to avoid bumping into people. She had no idea how long she could hang on to this invisibility, so she moved fast, tearing into Jenna's bedroom. The teddy bear was on the bed.

Back out in the hallway, she ran into the stairwell. Jenna didn't look in her direction, so she knew she must still be invisible. She closed her eyes. *I want to come back, I want to come back. Tracey, let's be real.*

'You did it!'

Amanda opened her eyes to see Jenna gaping at her in admiration. She thrust the teddy bear into Jenna's arms. 'Let's get out of here.'

Once they were out of Brookside Towers, Amanda turned to Jenna. 'You're going to have to do something about this, you know.'

'About what?'

'Your mother, how you're living – all that.'

'You can't tell anyone, Amanda. This is even more important than the teddy bear. Do you know what would happen to me if people found out about my mother?'

Amanda could guess. 'They'd take you away from her and put you in some kind of foster care.'

Jenna nodded.

'There must be someone who can help you,'

Amanda said. 'What about Madame? I get the feeling she really cares about us – I mean, about you guys.' She couldn't believe she'd said 'us', like she was actually one of them.

Jenna shook her head. 'I can't take the chance. She might feel like she has to tell the authorities.' She shook her head ruefully. 'Isn't this weird? You, Amanda Beeson – you're the only one who knows about my life. And I actually trust you.'

'Yeah, it's pretty weird all right,' Amanda replied. 'You're the only one who knows my secrets too. And I've got another favour to ask you. Could you please never try to read my mind without asking me first?'

'OK,' Jenna said.

'Thanks.'

After a moment, Jenna said, 'Now you tell me something. Are we friends?'

'I wouldn't go that far,' Amanda said. 'But . . . we're not enemies.'

Jenna nodded. 'Yeah, I know what you mean.'

Amanda was pleased that Jenna understood. She really couldn't picture herself-as-herself hanging out with Jenna Kelley.

But on the other hand, she might be Tracey Devon for a long, long time. And considering Tracey's general unpopularity, she'd need all the friends she could get.

CHAPTER FIFTEEN

I T SEEMED TO JENNA that Amanda had found herself in a pretty nice place in the Devon household. She corrected herself – Amanda had *made* herself a nice place. From what she'd learned, life hadn't been like this for poor Tracey. According to Amanda, Tracey had been ignored in this family, virtually invisible even when she was visible.

Looking around now, Jenna found it difficult to believe this had ever been the case. At the big, round breakfast table, the septuplets argued over who would get to sit on either side of their big sister.

Mrs Devon hovered over her. 'Tracey, you absolutely must have more French toast. You need to eat; you're way too thin. Do you have your lunch money? Jenna, dear, please make sure Tracey eats her lunch at school.'

'Yes, Mrs Devon,' Jenna said. Boy, was Tracey in for a shock when she got back into her own body! she thought. Amanda had made Tracey's presence known.

She mentioned this to Amanda as they set off for the bus stop.

'It wasn't that hard,' Amanda told her. 'Tracey must be a complete wimp to put up with her parents behaving like that. She needs to stand up for herself and make demands. I just hope she can keep this up when she comes back, and she doesn't fade away again.'

'You won't let her do that,' Jenna assured her.

Amanda frowned. 'What's that supposed to mean? Once we're back in our own bodies, I guarantee you I won't be involved with Tracey Devon.'

'You don't feel like you're kind of connected now?'

'No!'

Her violent response almost made Jenna jump. 'Jeez, I'm not saying you guys have to be best friends or anything like that, but . . .'

The bus was coming. 'Watch this,' Amanda said. 'This bus driver never noticed her before. Sometimes he closed the door in her face.' This time, when the doors opened, Amanda was the first to climb on, and the driver actually said 'Good morning' to her.

They sat down. 'Look,' Amanda said, 'I'm doing what I can to make Tracey's life better. And if I say so myself, she's less of a nerd than she was before I got my hands on her. But when this business is over, don't imagine I'm ever going to be hanging out with Tracey Devon. We live in completely different worlds. Could you even imagine Tracey with the real me and my friends?'

'Wow, you really *are* a snob,' Jenna commented.

Amanda shrugged. 'Like I care what you think of me.'

'I don't get it,' Jenna said. 'Sometimes I feel like you're really an OK person, and then you turn around and act like this.'

'I'm practising so I'll be ready when I'm myself again,' Amanda informed her.

Jenna sighed and sank back into her seat. Popular girls had always been a mystery to her, and getting to know Amanda hadn't helped her understand them any better. And even though she'd promised Amanda she wouldn't read her mind without asking first, she couldn't resist. She closed her eyes and concentrated.

I hope she finds a new mother's help this week. I want her to take me shopping on Saturday. I don't really mind babysitting the kids. Sandie and Mandie are funny, and I feel especially close to Randie. I can't hate them — it's not their fault I don't get enough attention. It's my parents' fault, and my own fault too.

Jenna was puzzled. 'She' was obviously Mrs Devon. But who was 'I'? Then she gasped.

'What?' Amanda asked.

'Look, don't get angry, but I just read some thoughts.'

Amanda was clearly annoyed. 'Hey, you promised—'

'Wait,' Jenna interrupted. 'I don't think they were *your* thoughts. I think I was hearing Tracey!'

Amanda's eyes widened. 'Really? What was she thinking? Is she getting ready to come back out?'

'It was something about how she wants her mother to take her shopping on Saturday. And some stuff about the little sisters, and how she really likes Randie.'

Amanda's face fell. 'Oh.'

'I thought you'd be pleased! If I can read Tracey's thoughts, she's got to be closer to the surface, right?'

'They weren't Tracey's thoughts,' Amanda told her glumly. 'They were mine.'

Jenna drew in her breath sharply. 'Ohmigod! Do you know what this could mean? You and Tracey . . . Maybe you're merging. You know, becoming one person together. Tracey-Amanda Devon-Beeson. Wow! What a name!'

'Shut up!' Amanda hissed furiously. 'Just shut your stupid mouth.'

Jenna wasn't offended by Amanda's sharp tongue. She thought she was beginning to understand now. Amanda was scared.

When they arrived at school the two girls parted, but Jenna didn't stop thinking about Amanda. In a way, she almost hoped her suspicions would turn out to be true – that Tracey was absorbing Amanda or vice versa. Because she had to admit, she kind of liked Amanda. She envied her confidence, and she admired the way Amanda was turning Tracey's life around.

And Amanda had ignited a tiny little hope in Jenna – that in the Amanda-style Tracey she might have found a friend who could help her improve her own life.

Amanda's mood seemed to have improved somewhat when they met again in the gifted class.

'I think I'm going to volunteer to be Serena's subject today,' she confided in Jenna.

'You're kidding! I told you, she doesn't give a damn about us – she just wants to use us.'

'I know,' Amanda said. 'She's definitely creepy. But I'm wondering if maybe hypnosis could be the answer. Like, if she went deep enough into my unconscious she'd have to find Tracey, right?'

'I don't know,' Jenna said. 'I guess it's worth a try.' But she had serious doubts that the student teacher would be able to do anything meaningful. Ken came in and took the seat next to her. Jenna turned to him.

'What happened when you had your meeting with Serena?' she asked.

Amanda turned to listen too.

He grinned. 'It was total bull. She was trying to get me to contact her great-grandmother to find out where she hid her jewellery before she died.'

Jenna gave Amanda a triumphant look. 'See? She's only looking out for herself. She's not going to help you.'

'Help you with what?' Ken asked Amanda.

'Nothing – nothing at all. Forget it and mind your own business,' Amanda snapped, while shooting a fierce look at Jenna. Jenna was more interested in watching Ken's reaction to Amanda's response. He was obviously startled, and Jenna couldn't blame him. That outburst was not a typical Tracey reaction.

As it turned out, Amanda didn't have the opportunity to volunteer anyway. The student teacher didn't come to class that day.

'Where's Serena?' Jenna asked Madame.

'I believe she called in sick,' Madame said. She actually seemed a little concerned, which Jenna thought was odd. She tried to figure out what Madame was really thinking, but as usual she couldn't get into her head.

'Is she seriously sick?' Jenna asked.

'No, just a cold. At least, that's what Principal Jackson told me.' The bell rang, and now she looked even more worried. 'Where is Emily?'

Nobody knew. Madame frowned.

'She's probably dawdling in the bathroom,' Amanda said. 'You know how she daydreams. Do you want me to go and get her?'

'No, that's all right,' Madame said. 'I'm sure she'll be along in a minute. Now, I would like us to spend our time today sharing some personal experiences. Usually we talk about how we've tried to suppress our gifts. I know this isn't always possible, and there may be times when it's appropriate to use them. So this time, let's talk about the positive ways you've used your gifts this week. Who'd like to go first?'

As usual, no hands shot up.

Madame sighed. 'All right, I'll decide who goes first. Martin?'

Martin looked frightened. 'I didn't do anything!'

'I don't intend to punish you, Martin. I just want to know if you did anything with your gift this week that you feel good about.'

Martin scrunched his little rat face as if he was thinking very hard. 'Oh, yeah . . . I was in the supermarket with my mother on Monday. And I saw this woman with a little kid – I guess he was about five – and he knocked something off a shelf. And his mother slapped him!'

'Oh dear,' Madame murmured. 'I don't approve of punishing children physically either. But what could you do about this, Martin? Did you say something to the woman?'

'Nah. I kicked her.'

'Martin!'

'Well, the little kid was too small to kick her himself. So I got even for him.'

Madame shook her head. 'Martin, how can you think that was a positive action?'

'Because I did it for the kid, not for myself! The woman wasn't hurt too badly – she just slid all the way down the aisle and looked really embarrassed. You should've seen the kid's face. He was really happy, so I felt good about myself.'

'How did you get away with it?' Charles wanted to know.

Martin beamed. 'I moved really fast, when no one was looking. And who's going to think someone like me could kick a person that far?'

Madame shook her head. 'I'm sorry, Martin, but I don't think this is a very good example of a positive action. Who can offer a better example?'

Sarah raised her hand, and Madame nodded in her direction.

'I saw a woman about to cross a street. Then a car came from around the corner, going way too fast, and the driver was talking on his mobile phone and not paying attention. He would have hit her if I hadn't made him hit the brakes.' She looked at the teacher pleadingly. 'I know I'm not supposed to interfere, Madame, but I couldn't let that poor woman get injured – maybe even killed!'

'That's cool,' Ken said. 'You saved her life.'

Jenna saw it another way. 'But maybe that woman was on her way to kill her husband. You would have saved *his* life if you'd let the car hit her.'

Sarah sighed and sank back into her chair.

Madame looked at Jenna reprovingly. 'Do *you* have an interesting story, Jenna?'

She didn't, but she managed to conjure up something. 'Um, the other day I was at the mall, and I knew some kids were planning to go in a store and steal stuff. They had it all worked out – they even had a gadget to take the security thingy off the items they swiped. So I told a security guard and they were arrested.'

It was only a little white lie, and she thought it would please Madame. Amanda turned around and raised her eyebrows, but Jenna ignored her.

'But how did you get the security guard to believe you?' Ken asked.

'That's a good question, Ken,' Madame said. 'We've talked about this before, Jenna. You all have to be very careful about revealing your abilities. What did you actually say to the guard?'

Jenna thought rapidly. 'I . . . I didn't say anything about mind reading. I told him I'd overheard the kids talking.'

Did Madame buy her story? Before she could respond the classroom door opened and the principal stuck his head in.

'Excuse me, Madame. Sorry to disturb your class,'

he droned. 'Just a message to relay. Emily Sanders is sick today.'

'Really?' Madame glanced at a sheet on her desk. 'She's not on the absentee list.'

'Secretary's error,' he said quickly and retreated, closing the door.

Madame stared after him. Then she shook her head, as if to shake out disturbing thoughts. 'Let's see, where were we? Who would like to share next? Charles?'

Jenna was relieved that Madame seemed to have forgotten *her* story. When Amanda-Tracey turned around, Jenna thought she wanted to congratulate her on getting away with that rewritten story. But the girl seemed to have something else on her mind.

'Emily's not sick. I saw her in the canteen earlier.'

'Maybe she got sick just before class,' Jenna suggested.

'Then why would the principal say it was a mistake that she wasn't on the absentee list?'

'Tracey?'

She had to turn back to face the teacher.

'Did you have a positive experience with your gift this week?'

'No.'

The teacher moved on to Ken, but Jenna had tuned out. Emily was still on her mind, and she couldn't shake her. It was like she was stuck in Jenna's head, and she didn't know why. So Emily was sick — so what? It was probably nothing serious, just a cold or something. Maybe she had thrown up that day's disgusting lunch.

Then why was she still in her head?

Jenna jerked as the answer came to her in a flash. She was thinking about Emily because Emily was trying to contact *her*.

But why would Emily want to communicate with Jenna? The answer was obvious: because Emily knew that Jenna could read minds. And she wanted Jenna to read hers, right that minute. But *why*?

Jenna shut her eyes and concentrated. *Emily . . . I'm listening. I'm trying to hear you. What do you want? Emily?*

Nothing . . . And then Emily began to fade from her mind. Another face replaced her — Serena, the student teacher.

This was getting even weirder. Why would Serena want to communicate with her? Was she having a problem getting Mr Jones to ask her out? And what did this have to do with Emily? Because now Emily was coming back into her head.

Emily was trying to tell her something about Serena. But it was all blurry and fuzzy, because, because . . . because Emily was under hypnosis.

The bell rang, and Jenna leaned forward. 'I have to tell you something,' she whispered.

'I don't understand,' Amanda said when she heard what had been going on in Jenna's mind. 'What does it mean?'

'Emily's trying to tell me something. I think she's in trouble. And it's something to do with Serena.'

'But Emily's at home sick, isn't she?'

Jenna wasn't so sure. 'Do you have a mobile?'

Amanda shook her head. 'That was the next thing I was going to tell Tracey's parents to give me.'

'Well, *I* don't have one.' Jenna regarded the passing stream of students and stopped. 'You've got one, don't you?'

'I just told you—'

'I mean, the *real* you.'

She looked practically offended by the question. 'Of course I do. Everyone who's anyone has a phone.'

Ignoring the insult, Jenna dashed down the hall and cornered Other-Amanda, who was standing at her locker with a couple of her snotty friends. 'I need to use your phone,' she declared.

'*What?*'

Jenna repeated her demand.

'Are you *serious*? Do you actually think that *I* would lend *you* my phone?' The two girls beside her looked horrified, as if Jenna was in the process of holding them up with a weapon. Which gave her an idea.

She moved in closer to Other-Amanda. 'Give me your phone,' she hissed, 'or I'll have my crew take care of you.'

One of the girls clutched Other-Amanda's arm. 'You'd better do it. She knows really bad people.'

But this Amanda was just as tough as the Amanda that Jenna knew. 'Forget it,' she snapped.

Fortunately her friends weren't quite so gutsy.

'Here, you can use mine,' the other one said, and thrust it into Jenna's hand.

Jenna dialled in the number for directory information. There were five Sanderses in the town, and Jenna told the operator to try the first one. There was no answer. No one answered the second one either, but on the third try she got someone.

'Hello?'

'Could I speak to Emily, please?'

'Emily's at school! Who is this?'

'Uh, wrong number.' She tossed the phone back to its owner, and ran back to Amanda.

'She's not at home, and I should have guessed that. She has to be nearby for me to be getting a message from her.'

'You think she's somewhere in this building?'

The images of Emily and Serena were coming faster and faster, and they were dark. 'Yeah. Let's start with the basement.'

The bell rang to signal the beginning of the next class. The two girls were heading for the stairs when a hall monitor appeared from around the corner and blocked their way.

'Where are your hall passes?'

Jenna had no patience for this nonsense. 'Get out of our way.'

The boy grabbed her arm with his right hand and Amanda's arm with his left. 'OK, you're both going to the office.'

Jenna struggled to free herself, but he was a big kid and he was strong. She turned to Amanda. '*Do something!*'

Amanda got the message. In less than a second, the hall monitor was holding nothing in his left hand. 'What the hell—?'

Jenna had hoped the shock of Amanda's disappearance would cause him to loosen his grip on her arm too, but he only tightened it. She barely felt it though, because now her head was actually hurting. Emily was trying very hard to reach her, and she knew something had to be terribly wrong.

But Jenna didn't have Martin's strength, or Charles's ability to move things, or Tracey's gift for becoming invisible. She wasn't Sarah – she couldn't force the guy to release her. All she had was the feeling that Emily needed help.

She'd have to count on Amanda to help her. Or Tracey. Or whoever was in that invisible body.

Chapter Sixteen

AMANDA HAD NEVER BEEN in that part of the lower level of the school. As far as she knew, it was nothing but storage rooms and plumbing and stuff like that. And she vaguely recalled signs directing a media club to meet down there, but only nerds belonged to clubs like that, so she wasn't sure.

One thing was clear – it was dark. And invisibility didn't seem to give her any special viewing powers.

Luckily she had no problem with her hearing. From down the hall, she picked up a faint whisper. As she edged closer, the voice became recognizable.

'You must do this, Emily. Keep your eyes on the red dot and listen to me. Think deeper . . . deeper.'

It was the student teacher. And even though Amanda had never had a session with Serena, she could guess that she was hypnotizing Emily. But why down here?

'The numbers are there, Emily. You can see them. Tell me the numbers.'

What she said didn't make any sense, but something about the tone made Amanda shiver.

'Listen to me, Emily. Can you hear me? Answer me, Emily.'

And then she heard Emily's voice, flat and expressionless. 'I can hear you.'

'Tell me the numbers!' There was more urgency in Serena's voice now. And it led Amanda right to the door.

They were in there – she knew that. What she didn't know was how she was going to get in there with them. In all her invisible experiences so far, doors had been open. Maybe she had the ability to pass through walls.

She pressed herself against the door. Her body didn't go through it, but it turned out that the door wasn't even completely closed. The next thing she knew, she was on the floor of the room.

'Who's there?' Serena asked sharply.

Still on the floor, Amanda looked up. It was a storage room, with stacks of chairs. Her eyes had become accustomed to the dark by now, and she saw Emily sitting in one of them. She knew she was still invisible, because Serena wasn't looking down at her but at the open door.

Serena moved to the door to shut it, and her foot touched Amanda's head in the process. 'Damn!' Serena muttered, and kicked the obstruction out of her way.

In her last conscious thought, Amanda learned something else about her condition. When you're invisible, you still *hurt*.

'Amanda?'

The voice seemed to be coming from very far away. Amanda strained to hear it. At least her head had stopped hurting.

'Amanda!'

The voice was sharp now. Amanda forced her eyes open. She was looking at Mr Jones, her history teacher.

'Amanda, I asked you a question. What were the

three main causes of the American Civil War?'

She'd read that chapter, she knew she had, but her brain wouldn't cooperate.

'Taxation without representation?'

Mr Jones looked at her in exasperation. 'That was the American Revolution, Amanda. Someone else? Britney?'

Amanda didn't hear Britney's response. She was gradually absorbing her circumstances.

Tracey had Ms Galvin for history. Mr Jones ... he was *her* history teacher. Amanda's history teacher. And that was what he'd just called her. Amanda.

She looked at her right hand. There it was – the tiny sapphire birthstone ring her parents had given her on her last birthday. And her Swatch watch was on her wrist. And the nails on her fingers weren't chewed down – they were rosy pink and manicured. She stared at them for what seemed like a long time.

'Amanda?' Mr Jones was speaking to her again.

'Yes?' she asked faintly, looking up at him.

Now he looked more concerned than annoyed. 'Are you feeling all right?'

'Yes ...' She was remembering. Emily sitting on a

chair. Serena. Something about numbers. 'No! I don't feel very well. I'd better go and see the school nurse.'

Mr Jones tore a hall pass off the pad on his desk, and Amanda snatched it from him on her race out of the classroom. Behind her, she could hear the class buzzing. They probably thought she was about to throw up. For once, Amanda didn't care what anyone thought about her.

She ran up the stairs, flapping the slip of paper at a passing hall monitor. Then she tore down the hall and burst into the gifted classroom.

Madame was alone in the room, pacing. When she heard Amanda come in, she whirled around with an expectant look on her face. When she saw Amanda, she seemed disappointed. 'Yes? Can I help you?'

'Emily's in trouble! You have to come with me!'

The teacher gasped. 'Who are you?'

The words tumbled out. 'I used to be Tracey. Tracey Devon. Emily's down in the basement with Serena, and—'

Madame didn't let her finish. She grabbed Amanda's arm. 'Take me to her!'

Rapidly Amanda led her down the two flights.

When they reached the basement, Serena's voice could be heard.

'The numbers, Emily! The numbers! I'm in control of your mind – you have to respond. What are the numbers?'

Then they could hear Emily's voice, not as loud, but distinct. 'Four . . . eighteen . . .'

'Yes, yes, keep going, I need all seven numbers.'

'Twenty-four . . .'

By now Madame had moved on ahead of Amanda, and she was the first to enter the storage room. Amanda was right behind her.

'Ms Hancock! What are you doing?'

'Get out of here!' the student teacher yelled. 'I'm working with a student!'

'Forty-six . . .' Emily murmured.

Madame strode forward and knocked the spinning disc out of Serena's hand. 'Wake up, Emily. Wake up!'

'Stop it! Stop it!' Serena shrieked. 'This is important! Keep going, Emily! Just three more numbers!'

But now Madame had her hands on Emily's

shoulders and was shaking her. Emily opened her eyes and smiled vaguely.

'Hello, Madame.'

'Emily, what's happening?'

'I'm predicting the winning lottery numbers. For next week.'

Madame looked fiercely at Serena and stepped towards her. Serena glared right back. 'Don't bother trying to report me. No one will believe you.'

Amanda tried to block the doorway as Serena started to walk out, but the student teacher pushed her aside. And Amanda didn't resist all that much. She didn't particularly want to know what might happen if she banged her head again.

It was when she stepped backwards that she almost tripped on something. No, some*body*. Madame saw her too.

'Tracey! Are you all right? What's going on?'

The thin, fair-haired girl struggled to her feet. 'I – I'm not sure.' She looked at Amanda, and her brow puckered. Then, a small smile appeared on her face.

'I know you . . .'

Amanda glared at her. 'No, you don't.' She turned

to Madame, who was now propping up a dazed Emily with one arm while reaching for Tracey with the other. 'I guess everything's OK here now, right?'

Without waiting for a response, she left the room, went back up to the main floor, and headed directly into a girls' bathroom. It was a long time since she'd fixed her hair and repaired her make-up.

CHAPTER SEVENTEEN

LUNCH WAS ALMOST OVER. From her prime seat at the best table, Amanda watched as students raced to the conveyor belt to dump their trays. She herself had no tray. *Someone* had not been watching her eating habits over the past week and had gained two pounds. Her mother had kindly prepared her a lunch of two hard-boiled eggs, carrot sticks and an apple.

Britney spoke. 'Ohmigod! Look at Terri Boyd.'

Amanda looked. 'What about her?'

'Her skirt's practically transparent. You can see her underwear.'

Amanda squinted. 'Oh yeah, right.'

Katie identified the next victim. 'See Cara Winters? She's been telling everyone she got that sweater from a J. Crew catalogue. But I saw the label when she took it off in PE and it came from Target.'

Amanda looked. 'Actually, you'd be surprised,' she remarked. 'They've got some pretty decent-looking clothes at Target.'

Katie, Britney, Nina, Sophie and Emma gaped at her in horror. 'When were *you* in Target?' Sophie asked.

Amanda grimaced. She'd been making stupid goofs like this for a couple of days. She had to remember who she was.

'Um, my mother was buying dish towels there. And we happened to walk past some clothes.'

They appeared to be satisfied with that explanation, though she could still see scepticism in Britney's expression. The old Amanda Beeson might have been forced to walk past the clothing department at Target, but she wouldn't have *looked* as she passed.

She didn't want to think that she'd changed at all over the last week, and she *certainly* didn't want her friends to notice anything different about her. But it wasn't always easy. Like right now, as Tracey Devon carried her tray past their table. Her eyes met Tracey's.

They didn't speak, but there was definitely a silent communication.

'Why are you looking at *her*?' Katie demanded to know.

Amanda couldn't resist. 'I was just wondering . . . Do you think she looks different?' she ventured.

'Yeah, I noticed that too,' Nina remarked. 'She's dressing a lot better. And I like her hair.'

'But she's still a nerd,' Britney reminded her. 'Once a nerd, always a nerd. And I'm absolutely positive *her* clothes came from Target.'

'Oh yes, absolutely,' Nina agreed.

They were right about *that*. Amanda remembered choosing the printed top to wear with that skirt. She was actually rather proud of her work.

'Why are we even talking about her?' Katie asked. 'She's nobody.'

'That's not true,' Amanda said. 'She's somebody.' Aware of how her friends were looking at her, she amended that. 'Just not somebody we want to know.'

She hadn't spoken to Tracey since that meeting in the basement storage room. She had to admit, she was curious. Where had Tracey been when

Amanda was in her body? Had she been aware of what was going on? Was her relationship with her parents still improving? And what about the Devon Seven? Amanda particularly wanted to know about Randie. Maybe someday, when no one was around to see, she could corner Tracey and get the answer to some ofher questions. And find out what Tracey remembered. And threaten her, or bribe her, or do whatever it took to make sure she never, ever told anyone what had happened.

Not that she was really worried. Who would believe it? Only one person other than herself knew the whole story – Jenna Kelley. And she knew Jenna would never tell. Because Jenna knew that Amanda had information that could send Jenna into foster care.

Or maybe she wouldn't tell because Jenna was actually a good person who wouldn't want to hurt Amanda . . . Amanda gritted her teeth. She hated when little thoughts like that popped into her head. They were so *not* Amanda-style thoughts.

Britney was looking at her oddly. 'You OK?'

'Fine,' Amanda said briskly. Knowing what she now knew about how Britney talked about her behind her back, Amanda was especially careful not to give her any clues about how she'd changed.

And there was another stupid not-Amanda thought. *I haven't changed. I'm me again.* 'I want to go to the bathroom and check my hair before the bell rings,' she announced.

Britney and Katie got up with their trays. 'We'll meet you there,' Katie announced.

She thought the bathroom was empty when she walked in, but then she heard a toilet flush, and Jenna Kelley came out of the stall.

She looked at Amanda, and Amanda looked at her. And Amanda couldn't stop herself. 'Are you still staying at Tracey's?'

'What's it to you?' Jenna snapped.

'Just wondering if that party's still going on at your place.'

Jenna glowered at her. 'Don't you *dare* feel sorry for me.'

'Don't worry,' Amanda said feelingly. 'I won't.'

Britney and Katie came in.

'How are things in vampireland, Jenna?' Britney asked, and Katie giggled.

Jenna walked out.

'Weirdo freak,' Britney murmured. 'Amanda, can I borrow your lipgloss?'

Amanda had history for her next class. She'd just walked in when Mr Jones beckoned her up to his desk.

'I just received a message,' he told her. 'You're wanted in administration.'

'Why?' Amanda asked, but Mr Jones didn't know. He handed her a hall pass and she left. When she entered the reception area, the secretary directed her to go directly into Mr Jackson's office.

The principal wasn't alone.

'Hello, Amanda,' Madame said.

Amanda froze.

The principal spoke. 'You're being transferred out of Mr Jones's class. Go with Madame.'

'But—'

'Come along, Amanda,' Madame said smoothly, and placed a gentle hand on her arm. Feeling like she'd stepped back into a nightmare, Amanda went along with her.

'It's not what you think,' she told the teacher frantically. 'You're making a mistake.'

Madame smiled. 'It'll be all right, Amanda. You'll see.'

They walked along in silence. 'Did you tell Mr Jackson about Serena?' she asked Madame.

Madame looked at her intently. 'It wouldn't make any difference, Amanda. She's disappeared.'

'Well, at least she won't be bothering Emily any more,' Amanda said.

Madame smiled again, but this time there was sadness behind the smile. 'Hopefully not. But there will always be another Serena.'

'There's going to be another student teacher?'

Madame rolled her eyes. 'No, I meant there will always be people who want something from my students. You'll have to be ready for that, Amanda. There's always going to be another threat. But I'm here to help you deal with them.'

As far as Amanda was concerned, the real threat lay just beyond the door of room 209.

* * *

They were all there in the gifted classroom – the eight strange students. Charles was still slumped sullenly in his wheelchair. The amnesia boy, Carter, wore the same blank expression. Little Martin was there, and Sarah, and Ken, and so was Emily, still looking dreamy and vague. Tracey watched her with interest, and Jenna had a little grin on her face. Knowing Jenna, Amanda figured it was a 'nyah, nyah' smirk.

'Have a seat, Amanda,' Madame said, pointing to the empty desk in front of Jenna and next to Ken. 'Class, we have a new student. Amanda Beeson.'

Ken looked at her in surprise. 'What are *you* doing here? Are you one of us?'

No! Amanda wanted to scream. *I'm Amanda Beeson, the coolest girl at Meadowbrook, the Queen of Mean, the girl who has it all!*

But there was no point in protesting. The cold, hard truth was evident, and she responded to Ken with a short nod.

She was Amanda Beeson. Another weirdo freak.

Nine secret gifts in one class —
what could possibly go wrong?

Find out over the page in an extract
from Book 2 in the Gifted series:

GIFTED
BETTER LATE
THAN NEVER

Chapter One

JENNA KELLEY STOOD at her bedroom window and gazed outside without really seeing anything. Not that there was much to see – just another dull brick building, exactly like her own. Sometimes Jenna could see people moving around in their apartments, but they rarely did anything worth watching.

It was a pretty dreary place, but it was home, and she wasn't thrilled with the prospect of leaving it. The grey skies and steady rain outside did nothing to improve her mood.

She turned away from the window and went to her chest of drawers. Taking up a stubby black pencil, she added another layer to the already thick line that circled her eyes, and stepped back to admire the effect. Kohl-rimmed eyes, short spiked hair, black

T-shirt, black jeans . . . no tattoos or piercings yet, but she had a stick-on fake diamond on her right nostril and it looked real. She hoped the way she looked would startle – maybe even shock – whoever she might be meeting.

In the mirror, behind her own reflection, she could see the empty suitcase lying open on her bed. Ignoring it, she left the room.

The sound of her footsteps on the bare floor echoed in the practically empty apartment. The silence gave her the creeps. She'd spent time alone here before, of course, but she'd always known her mother would show up before too long. This time it was different. Her mother would be staying in the hospital rehab centre for two weeks. Just knowing this made Jenna feel even more alone.

She considered turning on the TV for some companionship, but then remembered that all she'd hear would be static, and the screen would be a blur. Her mother hadn't paid the cable bill and the service had been cut off the previous week.

Instead she went into the kitchen and opened the refrigerator door, even though she knew there wouldn't be anything edible in there. She removed a half-empty bottle of cola. There was no fizz left, but it was better than nothing.

What was her mother doing right now? she wondered. Screaming at a nurse? Demanding a gin and tonic? Jenna wanted to be optimistic. Maybe her mother would make it this time, but she couldn't count on it. She'd tried to stop drinking before, but had never made it beyond a day or two. That very morning, before she left, she'd drained what was left in a bottle, then announced that this was the last alcohol she'd ever drink. Jenna had tried to read her mind, to get a more accurate picture of how serious and committed her mother was this time, but she couldn't get inside.

It was funny, when Jenna considered how easily she read minds. Young or old, male or female, clever or stupid – most people couldn't stop her from eavesdropping on their thoughts. But there were some who were just not accessible. Like her mother.

She used to think her mother's mind was too cloudy and messed up to penetrate. Then she thought that maybe there was another reason, like a blood connection, that prevented her from reading the mind of a family member. Unfortunately there were no other family members around, so she couldn't test that theory. She'd never known her father – according to her mother, he'd taken off before Jenna was even born. She had no brothers or sisters, and her mother had left her own family when she was young, so Jenna had never met any grandparents, aunts, uncles or cousins.

Eventually she realized that her inability to read her mother's mind wasn't caused by the family connection. Just six months ago, when she'd been placed in the special so-called 'gifted' class at Meadowbrook Middle School, she found that she couldn't read the mind of the teacher, a woman they called Madame. She'd tried and tried, but she was completely blocked from getting into the teacher's head, and she'd finally given up. Maybe it was because Madame knew all their gifts so well that she was somehow able to protect herself from the special students. Gifts . . . It was a strange way to describe their unique abilities, Jenna thought. She certainly didn't feel gifted.

A selected list of titles available from
Macmillan Children's Books

The prices shown below are correct at the time of going to press. However, Macmillan Publishers reserves the right to show new retail prices on covers, which may differ from those previously advertised.

Marilyn Kaye

Gifted: Better Late than Never	978-0-7534-16501	£5.99

Cathy Hopkins

Zodiac Girls: Dancing Queen	978-0-7534-1765-2	£5.99
Zodiac Girls: Discount Diva	978-0-7534-1503-0	£5.99

Malcom Rose

Traces: Framed!	978-0-7534-1493-4	£5.99
Traces: Lost Bullet	978-0-7534-1494-1	£5.99
Traces: Roll Call	978-0-7534-1495-8	£5.99

All Pan Macmillan titles can be ordered from our website, www.panmacmillan.com, or from your local bookshop and are also available by post from:

Bookpost, PO Box 29, Douglas, Isle of Man IM99 1BQ
Credit cards accepted. For details:
Telephone: 01624 677237
Fax: 01624 670 923
Email: bookshop@enterprise.net
www.bookpost.co.uk
Free postage and packing in the United Kingdom